I0651062

Anonymous

A Modern Symposium

Subjects: The soul and future life, by Frederic Harrison and, The influence upon

morality of a decline in religious belief, by Sir James Fitzjames Stephen

Anonymous

A Modern Symposium
Subjects: The soul and future life, by Frederic Harrison and, The influence upon morality of a decline in religious belief, by Sir James Fitzjames Stephen

ISBN/EAN: 9783337260088

Printed in Europe, USA, Canada, Australia, Japan

Cover: Foto ©Andreas Hilbeck / pixelio.de

More available books at **www.hansebooks.com**

A

MODERN SYMPOSIUM.

SUBJECTS:

THE SOUL AND FUTURE LIFE.

BY

FREDERIC HARRISON, R. H. HUTTON, PROF. HUXLEY,
LORD BLACHFORD, HON. RODEN NOEL, LORD
SELBORNE, CANON BARRY, MR. W. R.
GREG, REV. BALDWIN BROWN,
DR. W. G. WARD;

AND

THE INFLUENCE UPON MORALITY OF A DECLINE IN RELIGIOUS BELIEF.

BY

SIR JAMES FITZJAMES STEPHEN, LORD SELBORNE, DR.
MARTINEAU, MR. FREDERIC HARRISON, THE DEAN
OF ST. PAUL'S, THE DUKE OF ARGYLL, PROF.
CLIFFORD, DR. WARD, PROF. HUXLEY,
MR. R. H. HUTTON.

Detroit:
ROSE-BELFORD PUBLISHING COMPANY.
1878.

CONTENTS.

PREFACE TO THIS EDITION.

A PROFOUND change, the signs of which are so legible that he who runs may read, but the end whereof it is hard to foresee, is coming over the religious belief of Christendom. One of the elements of this metamorphosis is a growing tendency towards logical consistency. It is becoming more and more generally seen that in religion man has but two guides, Reason and Authority; that the two are fundamentally antagonistic, but that either may be adopted without landing us in irreconcilable contradictions: in other words, that a searcher after religious truth must do one of two things—either submit himself unreservedly to the control of an Authority claiming to be divine and infallible, or follow Reason whithersoever it leads, regardless of consequences, which may be safely left to take care of themselves. The intellectual leaders of the age—the John Stuart Mills and the Herbert Spencers—are naturally found on the one side; while the submissive flocks who in all times and countries have rejoiced the hearts of all priesthoods, whether Brahmin, Buddhist, Christian, or Mohammedan, as inevitably gravitate to the other. These two opposite tendencies are evidenced, on the one hand, by a very no-

ticeable growth of Roman Catholicism and Ritualism in
England and the United States ; and, on the other, by an
even more remarkable spread of infidelity, and by the increasing influence of rationalistic parties within the
orthodox Churches themselves.　People are year by year
becoming more alive to the fact that Reason and Authority are radically opposed, that the conflict between
them is a life and death struggle, that an absolute choice
must be made of one or the other, and that all attempts
at compromise, such as that sought by Evangelical Prot-
estantism, which in one breath proclaims the thoroughly
rationalistic doctrine of the right of private judgment,
and in the next seeks to fetter the free action of the
human mind by confining it within the shackles of iron-
clad creeds and confessions of faith, made three or four
hundred years ago by fallible mortals like ourselves, are
essentially irrational and doomed to inevitable failure.
In the English Church the three parties are represented
by the High Church, with the Ritualists at the extreme
wing ; the Broad Church, or Rationalisers ; and the Low
Church, or Evangelicals : or, as some irreverent wit has
christened them, the Attitudinarians, the Latitudinarians,
and the Platitudinarians.

The Churches of Authority, whether Roman, Ritualist,
or High Anglican, and the Churches of Compromise,
whether Lutheran, Low Anglican, Presbyterian, Metho-
dist, or Baptist, need no more than a passing allusion here.
They are merely seeking to walk in the old paths. *Semper
eadem* might be chosen as their motto by all, as it has been

by one of them. It is when we come to the other section
of the religious world,—to those who, with a single eye
to TRUTH, choose Reason as their guide, and follow it to
its logical outcome,—that we see how vast is the change
that is coming over the belief of Christendom. It is not
merely that such subjects as the inspiration of the Bible,
the divinity of Christ, the existence of Hell, and the doctrines of the Atonement and Eternal Damnation are being
questioned with a vigour and pertinacity to which the
past affords no parallel. These dogmas were questioned
by Voltaire and Paine and the other Deists of the eigh-
teenth century. The change is even more fundamental :
it is, in the extremest sense, radical; so that a book which
caused so great a ferment when it originally appeared as
" The Age of Reason," would, were it now published for
the first time, create so little remark as almost to fall
still-born from the press. Intellectual Christendom has
travelled a long way since that work was written.
Among the subjects now being discussed with a keenness
and searching rigour unknown in former times are questions so fundamental as the existence and personality of
God, and the existence and immortality of the human
soul. Reason is doing its work thoroughly ; it is digging
down to the very foundations of religion, with the full
and passionate determination that the faith of the future
—be it Neo-Christianity or any other—shall be founded
on a rock, not on a quicksand. The Reformation of the
nineteenth century is an infinitely more portentous phenomenon than its forerunner of the sixteenth. It is no

mere reform. The question now is, whether Christianity shall continue to exist, even with such radical changes as will make it virtually a new thing; or whether it shall be replaced by an altogether new edifice built upon a scientific foundation of positive, verifiable truth.

The leading subject dealt with in this volume is one of those root questions above referred to, which lie at the bottom of all religion—the existence and immortality of the human soul. The present discussion is perhaps the noblest, as it is certainly the weightiest contribution towards the solution of the momentous question at issue that has ever appeared in print, not even excepting the immortal "Phædo" of Plato; and the numerous incidental direct or indirect allusions to it which have been made on this continent as well as in England, are proofs of the profound impression which it has created. Nor is this widespread interest a matter for wonder. To every human being who can at times lift himself above the cares and trivialities of this life, the question, "If a man die, shall he live again?" must ever be the most solemn and heart-searching. It would, of course, be absurd to pretend that "the Great Enigma" is at last solved. Probably it is insoluble; or, at least, will remain so until the alleged facts of Spiritualism are proved beyond cavil, of which there appears to be no immediate prospect; or until some "traveller" from that "undiscovered country" of which Hamlet speaks so mournfully, returns and tells us of his wanderings, and of the glories and joys, and mayhap also the sorrows, of that unknown land. But if

the problem *be* insoluble it is well to know even so much ;
it is well to recognise that man is not a god, that his capacities are not infinite, and that it is mere childish-
ness perversely to war against the established limits of
his intelligence. We shall then concern ourselves with
matters within the scope of our powers, and cease to
waste our energies in vain repinings because we cannot
pierce behind a veil, which, if it be impenetrable, we can
at least believe has been made so for some wise and holy
purpose. If the discussion which is here reprinted leads
only to this result, it will not have been had in vain.

The other subject touched upon in this volume—the
influence upon morality of a decline in religious belief—is
one which would inevitably come up for discussion in
a time of religious transition. Such periods have
always been marked by a certain amount of moral
laxity. The age of the Reformation was so, as witness
the excesses of the Anabaptists and other fanatics and
enthusiasts of that day; and something of the same sort
may be in store for us now. It seems self-evident that a
weakening in the foundation must lead to a weakening
in the superstructure ; and where morality is based upon
religion, as to a large extent it is with Christianity, anything which affects the latter must inevitably react upon
the former. But the evil will be only temporary, and
will be more than compensated by a greater good. Morality must gain in the end by being placed upon a true
foundation instead of a false one. If the result of the
present yeasty ferment be the evolution of a new religion,

that religion will, we may be sure, be truer and better than the old one; and the morality based upon it must share in the benefit. But the question among scientific moralists now is, whether morality shall not be altogether removed from off its old religious foundation, and placed upon one of its own, to wit, the human conscience, with the well-being of man and all other sentient creatures for its aim. To the scientific moralist it seems better that a man should refrain from doing an evil act because he himself knows or feels it to be evil, rather than because some one else tells him it is evil; and, on the other hand, that it will be a gain to get rid of the false idea—if it be a false one—that the human conscience is, in some peculiar and special sense, the voice of God and therefore infallible, and replace it by the true idea—if it be a true one—that the conscience is a mere human faculty, imperfect like the rest of man's faculties, In infallibility there are no degrees, so that, if the former theory be true, the conscience of a Feejee Island savage or a Bushman is on a level with that of a Buddha or a Plato. Both are equally divine, both equally infallible. If, however, the rival theory be true, that the conscience is a human faculty in precisely the same sense that the intellect and the æsthetic instinct are human faculties, it follows that the moral sense—or that power, by whatever name it is called, by which we judge an act to be right or wrong— is more developed in the civilized man than in the savage, just as it is more developed in the man than in the child; and that even in the civilized *man* it is finite, imperfect, fallible, and consequently susceptible of education, improvement, progress, evolution. It is obvious that a searching enquiry into the relation of morality to religion must be of the gravest practical importance in a time of such vital change as that in which we live.

Both questions treated of in these pages are discussed from widely different standpoints, ranging from Roman Catholicism at the one extreme to Positivism at the other. One feature of the controversy might well be imitated on this side of the Atlantic—that is, the noble tolerance, gentleness, and courtesy shown towards the most opposite views, however manifestly distasteful. The nearest approach to warmth of temper occurs, curiously enough, in the vigorous passage-at-arms between Mr. Harrison and Professor Huxley, who, on the general question, are almost at one. The discussions, or "Symposia," originally appeared in the *Nineteenth Century*, a monthly review recently started in London, under the editorship of Mr. James Knowles, formerly editor of the *Contemporary*. A brief sketch of the different contributors or disputants may not be without interest to readers in this country.

Mr. Frederic Harrison is one of the leaders of the English Positivists or Comtists, and one of the ablest review-writers now living. He has been for years a prominent contributor to the *Fortnightly* and other reviews, on political, economical, and theological questions. A number of his essays were recently collected and published in book form. He has also published a translation of

" Social Statics," being the second volume of Comte's
" Positive Polity."

Mr. Richard Holt Hutton is the editor of the London
Spectator, and the author of a number of literary and
theological essays which were published in 1871 in two
volumes. He is one of the subtlest literary critics of the
day, his masterly essay on Goethe, in particular, having
been pronounced by high authority to be the finest piece
of biographical criticism that exists in any language. In
theology he is Broad-Church, of the school of the late
F. D. Maurice.

Professor Huxley is well-known as one of the greatest
of living biologists and one of the ablest expounders of
popular science. Of his numerous works the best known
are his " Lay Sermons, Addresses, and Reviews," published
in 1870, and his " Critiques and Addresses," published in
1873. In science he is an uncompromising advocate of
the Darwinian theory, and of Evolution in general ; in
philosophy he is a sensationalist of the school of Locke,
Descartes, Mill, and Spencer ; and in religion apparently
holds the new and growing creed of Agnosticism.

Lord Blachford, better known as Sir Frederick Rogers,
is a lawyer by profession, having been called to the English bar in 1836. He was Permanent Under-Secretary of
State for the Colonies, from 1860 till 1871, when he was
appointed Privy Councillor, and raised to the peerage
under the title of Baron Blachford.

The Hon. Roden Noel is a son of the first Earl of

Gainsborough, was born in 1834, and educated at Trinity College, Cambridge, where he took his degree in 1858. He was groom to the Privy Chamber of Her Majesty from 1867 to 1871. He is a voluminous writer, and his poetry is highly spoken of.

Lord Selborne, formerly Sir Roundell Palmer, acquired his present title when made Lord-Chancellor in 1872. He was one of the counsel on behalf of the English Government in the arbitration at Geneva, on the Alabama claims. He edited the well-known "Book of Praise, from the best English Hymn writers," published in 1862.

Canon Barry is the author of numerous works, including an "Introduction to the Old Testament;" "Notes on the Gospels;" "Life of Sir C. Barry;" "Cheltenham College Sermons;" "Notes on the Catechism;" and "Religion for Every Day: Lectures to Men." He was Head Master of Leeds Grammar School for eight years; in 1862 was appointed Principal of Cheltenham College, in 1868 Principal of King's College, London, and in 1871 a Canon of Worcester. He is a son of Sir Charles Barry, the eminent architect.

Mr. William Rathbone Greg is one of the best known and most eloquent theological writers of the day. His "Creed of Christendom," though written over thirty years ago, still ranks as the ablest work of its kind in the language; so able indeed that no satisfactory reply to it has ever been forthcoming; a fact which, as Mr. F. W. Newman has remarked, goes far to show that it is unanswerable. His other works are "Enigmas of Life;" "Literary and Social Judgments;" "Political Problems;" "Essays on Political and Social Science;" and "Rocks Ahead." Mr. Greg was a member of the English Civil Service, having been appointed a Commissioner of Customs in 1856; and Controller of Her Majesty's Stationery Office, in 1864, an office from which he retired last year.

The Rev. James Baldwin Brown is a leading Independent clergyman, of Brixton, London; and a voluminous author. His principal works are "The Home Life in the Light of its Divine Idea," which has passed through five editions; "The Divine Life in Man;" "The Soul's Exodus and Pilgrimage;" "The Christian Policy of Life;" "The Higher Life: its Reality, Experience, and Destiny;" and "The Doctrine of Annihilation, in the Light of the Gospel of Love." In theology he belongs to the liberal or "broad" school.

Dr. W. G. Ward is a leading Roman Catholic writer, and the editor of the *Dublin Review*, a quarterly, and the ablest Roman Catholic periodical published in the English language.

Sir James Fitzjames Stephen is one of the ablest jurists in England, and the author of "The Law of Evidence;" "The Indian Evidence Act;" and other legal works; also of a notable work on "Liberty, Equality, and Fraternity," intended as an answer to Mill's famous essay on Liberty.

The Rev. James Martineau is a leading clergyman of the Unitarian denomination, and was appointed Principal of Manchester New College, London, in 1868. He is the author of numerous works, including, among many others, " The Rationale of Religiou♥ Enquiry ; " " Studies of Christianity ; " " Essays, Philosophical and Theological ; " and " Religion as affected by Modern Materialism." He was one of the founders of the *National Review*. In 1875 the University of Leyden conferred upon him the honorary degree of D.D. He is a brother of the late Harriet Martineau.

The Dean of St. Paul's (the Very Rev. Richard William Church) was born in 1815, educated at Oxford, and took his degree in 1836. In 1854 he published a volume of essays which at once established his reputation as a scholarly and graceful writer. Two of these essays were afterwards expanded into a separate volume, and published under the title of " The Life of St. Anselm." In 1869 he published a volume of Sermons on the relation of Christianity to Civilization; and he is also the author of the " Sacred Poetry of Early Religions." He was appointed Dean of St. Paul's in 1871.

The Duke of Argyll is a prominent Scottish Liberal statesman, having been a member of several administrations, the last office held by him being Secretary of State for India, in Mr. Gladstone's Cabinet. He is also well known as the author of an able work on " The Reign of Law," which has passed through many editions ; and a

small work on " Primeval Man." In 1861 he was elected
President of the Royal Society of Edinburgh. In 1871 his
eldest son, the Marquis of Lorne, married the Princess
Louise.

Prof. Clifford is a mathematician by profession, and
a frequent contributor to the *Fortnightly* and other
reviews. In theology he may perhaps fairly be classed
with the Positivist school.

F. T. J.

Toronto, *2nd April, 1878.*

THE SOUL AND FÚTURE LIFE.

FREDERIC HARRISON.

HOW many men and women continue to give a mechanical acquiescence to the creeds, long after they have parted with all definite theology, out of mere clinging to some hope of a future life, in however dim and inarticulate a way! And how many, whose own faith is too evanescent to be put into words, profess a sovereign pity for the practical philosophy wherein there is no place for their particular yearning for a heaven to come! They imagine themselves to be, by virtue of this very yearning, beings of a superior order, and, as if they inhabited some higher zone amid the clouds, they flout sober thought as it toils in the plain below; they counsel it to drown itself in sheer despair or take to evil living, they rebuke it with some sonorous household word from the Bible or the poets—" Eat, drink, for to-morrow ye die "—" Were it not better not to be ?" And they assume the question closed when they have murmured triumphantly, " Behind the veil—behind the veil."

2

They are right, and they are wrong: right to cling to a hope of something that shall endure beyond the grave; wrong in their rebukes to men who in a different spirit cling to this hope as earnestly as they. We too turn our thoughts to that which is behind the veil. We strive to pierce its secret with eyes, we trust, as eager and as fearless; and even it may be more patient in searching for the realities beyond the gloom. That which shall come *after* is no less solemn to us than to you. We ask you, therefore: What do you *know* of it? Tell us; we will tell you what we hope. Let us reason together in sober and precise prose. Why should this great end, staring at all of us along the vista of each human life, be forever a matter for dithyrambic hypotheses and evasive tropes? What in the language of clear sense does any one of us hope for after death: what precise kind of life, and on what grounds? It is too great a thing to be trusted to poetic ejaculations, to be made a field for Pharisaic scorn. At least be it acknowledged that a man may think of the soul and of death and of future life in ways strictly positive (that is, without ever quitting the region of evidence), and yet may make the world beyond the grave the centre to himself of moral life. He will give the spiritual life a place as high, and will dwell upon the promises of that which is after death as confidently as the believers in a celestial resurrection. And he can do this without trusting his all to a *perhaps* so vague that a spasm of doubt can wreck it, but trusting, rather, to a mass of solid knowledge, which no man of any school denies to be true so far as it goes.

I.

THERE ought to be no misunderstanding at the outset
as to what we who trust in positive methods mean by the
word "soul," or by the words "spiritual," "materialist," and
"future life." We certainly would use that ancient and
beautiful word soul, provided there be no misconception
involved in its use. We assert as fully as any theologian
the supreme importance of spiritual life. We agree with
the theologians that there is current a great deal of real
materialism, deadening to our higher feeling. And we
deplore the too common interference to the world beyond
the grave. And yet we find the centre of our religion
and our philosophy in man and man's earth.

To follow out this use of old words, and to see that
there is no paradox in thus using them, we must go back
a little to general principles. The matter turns altogether
upon habits of thought. What seems to you so shocking
will often seem to us so ennobling, and what seems to us
flimsy will often seem to you sublime, simply because our
minds have been trained in different logical methods;
and hence you will call that a beautiful truth which
strikes us as nothing, but a random guess. It is idle, of
course, to dispute about our respective logical methods,
or to pit this habit of mind in a combat with that. But
we may understand each other better if we can agree to
follow out the moral and religious temper, and learn that
it is quite compatible with this or that mental procedure.

It may teach us again that ancient truth, how much human nature there is in men; what fellowship there is in our common aspirations and moral forces; how we all live the same spiritual life; while the philosophies are but the ceaseless toil of the intellect seeking again and again to *explain* more clearly that spiritual life, and to furnish it with reasons for the faith that is in it.

This would be no place to expound or to defend the positive method of thought. The question before us is simply, if this positive method has a place in the spiritual world or has anything to say about a future beyond the grave. Suffice it that we mean by the positive method of thought (and we will now use the term in a sense not limited to the social construction of Comte) that method which would base life and conduct, as well as knowledge, upon such evidence as can be referred to logical canons of *proof*, which would place all that occupies man in a homogenous system of *law*. On the other hand, this method turns aside from *hypotheses* not to be tested by any known logical canon familiar to science, whether the hypothesis claims support from intuition, aspiration or general plausibility. And, again, this method turns aside from ideal standards which avow themselves to be *lawless*, which profess to transcend the field of law. We say, life and conduct shall stand for us wholly on a basis of law, and must rest entirely in that region of science (not physical but moral and social science) where we are free to use our intelligence in the methods known to us as intelligible logic, methods which the intellect can analyze.

When you confront us with hypotheses, however sublime
and however affecting, if they cannot be stated in terms
of the rest of our knowledge, if they are disparate to that
world of sequence and sensation which to us is the ultimate base of all our real knowledge, then we shake our
heads and turn aside. I say, turn aside; and I do not
say, dispute. We cannot *disprove* the suggestion that
there are higher channels to knowledge in our aspirations
or our presentiments, as there might be in our dreams
by night as well as by day; we courteously salute the
hypotheses, as we might love our pleasant dreams; we
seek to prove no negatives. We do not pretend there are
no mysteries; we do not frown on the poetic splendours of
the fancy. There is a world of beauty and of pathos in
the vast ether of the Unknown in which this solid ball
hangs like a speck. Let all who list, who have true
imagination and not mere paltering with a loose fancy
—let them indulge their gift, and tell us what their
soaring has unfolded. Only let us not waste life in crude
dreaming, or loosen the knees of action. For life and
conduct, and the great emotions which react on life and
conduct, we can place nowhere but in the same sphere of
knowledge, under the same canons of proof, to which we
intrust all parts of our life. We will ask the same
philosophy which teaches us the lessons of civilization to
guide our lives as responsible men; and we go again to
the same philosophy which orders our lives to explain to
us the lessons of death. We crave to have the supreme
hours of our existence lighted up by thoughts and motives,

such as we can measure beside the common acts of our daily existence, so that each hour of our life up to the grave may be linked to the life beyond the grave as one continuous whole, " bound each to each by natural piety." And so, wasting no sighs over the incommensurable possibilities of the fancy, we will march on with a firm step till we knock at the gates of death ; bearing always the same human temper, in the same reasonable beliefs, and with the same earthly hopes of prolonged activity among our fellows, with which we set out gayly in the morning of life.

When we come to the problem of the human soul, we simply treat man as man, and we study him in accordance with our human experience. Man is a marvellous and complex being, we may fairly say of complexity past any hope of final analysis of ours, fearfully and wonderfully made to the point of being mysterious. But incredible progress has been won in reading this complexity, in reducing this mystery to order. Who can say that man shall ever be anything but an object of awe and of unfathomable pondering to himself ? Yet he would be false to all that is great in him, if he decried what he already has achieved toward self-knowledge.   Man has probed his own corporeal and animal life, and is each day arranging it in more accurate adjustment with the immense procession of animal life around him.   He has grouped the intellectual powers, he has traced to their relations the functions of mind, and ordered the laws of thought into a logic of a regular kind.   He has analyzed and grouped

the capacities of action, the moral faculties, the instincts
and emotions. And not only is the analysis of these
tolerably clear, but the associations and correlations of
each with the other are fairly made manifest. At the
lowest, we are all assured that every single faculty of man
is capable of scientific study. Philosophy simply means,
that every part of human nature acts upon a method, and
does not act chaotically, inscrutably, or in mere caprice.

But then we find throughout man's knowledge of himself signs of a common type. There is organic unity in
the whole. These laws of the separate functions, of body,
mind, or feeling, have visible relations to each other, are
inextricably woven in with each other, act and react,
depend and interdepend, one on the other. There is no
such thing as an isolated phenomenon, nothing *sui
generis*, in our entire scrutiny of human nature. Whatever the complexities of it, there is through the whole a
solidarity of a single unit. Touch the smallest fibre of
the corporeal man, and in some infinitesimal way we may
watch the effect in the moral man, and we may trace this
effect up into the highest pinnacles of the spiritual life.
On the other hand, when we rouse chords of the most
glorious ecstasy of the soul, we may see the vibration of
them, visibly thrilling upon the skin. The very animals
about us can perceive the emotion. Suppose a martyr
nerved to the last sacrifice, or a saint in the act of reliev-
ing a sufferer, the sacred passion within him is stamped
in the eye, or plays about the mouth, with a connection
as visible as when we see a muscle acting on a bone, or

the brain affected by the supply of blood. Thus from the summit of spiritual life to the base of corporeal life, whether we pass up or down the gamut of human forces, there runs one organic correlation and sympathy of parts. Man is one, however compound. Fire his conscience and he blushes. Check his circulation, and he thinks wildly, or he thinks not at all. Impair his secretions, and moral sense is dulled, discoloured, or depraved ; his aspirations flag, his hope, love, faith reel. Impair them still more, and he becomes a brute. A cup of drink degrades his moral nature below that of a swine. Again, a violent emotion of pity or horror makes him vomit. A lancet will restore him from delirium to clear thought. Excess of thought will waste his sinews. Excess of muscular exercise will deaden thought. An emotion will double the strength of his muscles. And at last the prick of a needle or a grain of mineral will in an instant lay to rest forever his body and its unity, and all the spontaneous activities of intelligence, feeling, and action, with which that compound organism was charged.

These are the obvious and ancient observations about the human organism. But modern philosophy and science have carried these hints into complete explanations. By a vast accumulation of proof positive, thought at last has established a distinct correspondence between every process of thought or of feeling and some corporeal phenomenon. Even when we cannot explain the precise relation, we can show that definite correlations exist. To positive methods, every fact of thinking reveals itself as having functional relations with molecular change. Every fact of will or of feeling is in similar relation with kindred molecular facts. And all these facts, again, have some relation to each other. Hence we have established an organic correspondence in all'manifestations of human life. To think implies a corresponding adjustment of molecular activity. To feel emotion implies nervous organs of feeling. To will implies vital cerebral hemispheres. Observation, reflection, memory, imagination, judgment have all been analyzed out, till they stand forth as functions of living organs in given conditions of the organism, that is in a particular environment. The whole range of man's powers, from the finest spiritual sensibility down to a mere automatic contraction, falls into one coherent scheme; being all the multiform functions of a living organism in presence of its encircling conditions.

But, complex as it is, there is no confusion in this whole when conceived by positive methods. No rational thinker now pretends that imagination is simply the vibration of a particular fibre. No man can *explain* volition by purely anatomical study. While keeping in view the due relations between moral and corporeal facts, we distinguish moral from biologic facts, moral science from biology. Moral science is based upon biological science; but it is not comprised in it; it has its own special facts and its own special methods, though always in the sphere of law. Just so the mechanism of the body is based upon mechanics, would be unintelligible but for mechanics, but could not be explained by mechanics alone, or by anything but a complete anatomy and biology. To explain the activity of the intellect as included in the activity of the body, is as idle as to explain the activity of the body as included in the motion of solid bodies. And it is equally idle to explain the activity of the will, or the emotions, as included in the theory of the intellect. All the spheres of human life are logically separable, though they are organically interdependent. Now the combined activity of the human powers organized around the highest of them we call the soul. The combination of intellectual and moral energy which is the source of religion, we call the spiritual life. The explaining the spiritual side of life by physical instead of moral and spiritual reasoning, we call materialism.

The consensus of the human faculties, which we call the soul, comprises all sides of human nature according to one homogeneous theory. But the intuitional methods ask us to insert into the midst of this harmonious system of parts, as an underlying explanation of it, an indescribable entity; and to this hypothesis, since the days of Descartes (or possibly of Aquinas), the good old word soul has been usually restricted. How and when this entity ever got into the organism, how it abides in it, what are its relations to it, how it acts on it, why and when it goes out of it—all is mystery. We ask for some evidence of the existence of any such entity; the answer is, we must imagine it in order to explain the organism. We ask what are its methods, its laws, its affinities; we are told that it simply has none, or none knowable. We ask for some description of it, of its course of development, for some single fact about it, statable in terms of the rest of our knowledge; the reply is—mystery, absence of everything so statable or cognizable, a line of poetry, or an ejaculation. It has no place, no matter, no modes, neither evolution nor decay : it is without body, parts or passions; a spiritual essence, incommensurable, incomparable, indescribable. Yet, with all this, it is, we are told, an entity, the most real and perfect of all entities short of the divine.

If we ask why we are to assume the existence of something of which we have certainly no direct evidence, and which is so wrapped in mystery that for practical purposes it becomes a nonentity, we are told that we need to conceive it, because a mere organism cannot act as we see the human organism act. Why not ? They say there must be a *principle* within as the cause of this life. But what do we gain by supposing a " principle ? " The " principle " only adds a fresh difficulty. Why should a " principle," or an entity, be more capable of possessing these marvelous human powers than the human organism? Besides we shall have to imagine a " principle " to explain not only why a man can feel affection, but also why a dog can feel affection. If a mother cannot love her child—merely *qua* human organism—unless her love be a manifestation of an eternal soul, how can a cat love her kittens—merely *qua* feline organism—without an immaterial principle or soul ? Nay, we shall have to go on to invent a principle to account for a tree growing, or a thunder-storm roaring, and for every force of Nature. Now this very supposition was made in a way by the Greeks, and to some extent by Aquinas, the author of the vast substructure of *anima* underlying all Nature, of which our human soul is the fragment that alone survives. One by one the steps in this series of hypothesis have faded away. Greek and mediæval philosophy imagined that every activity resulted not from the body which exhibited the activity, but from some mysterious entity inside it. If marble was hard, it had a " form " in forming its hardness; if a blade of grass sprang up, it had a vegetative spirit mysteriously impelling it; if a dog obeyed his master, it had an animal spirit mysteriously controlling its organs. The mediæval physicists, as Molière reminds us, thought that opium induced sleep *quia est in eo virtus dormitiva.* Nothing was allowed to act as it did by its own force or vitality. In every explanation of science we were told to postulate an intercalary hypothesis. Of this huge mountain of figment, the notion of man's immaterial soul is the one feeble residuum.

Orthodoxy has so long been accustomed to take itself for granted, that we are apt to forget how very short a period of human history this sublimated essence has been current. From Plato to Hegel the idea has been continually taking fresh shapes. There is not a trace of it in the Bible in its present sense, and nothing in the least akin to it in the Old Testament. Till the time of Aquinas theories of a material soul, as a sort of gas, were never eliminated; and until the time of Descartes, our present ideas of the antithesis of soul and body were never clearly defined. Thus the Bible, the Fathers, and the mediæval Church, as was natural when philosophy was in a state of flux, all represented the soul in very different ways ; and none of these ways were those of a modern divine. It is a curious instance of the power of words that the practical weight of the popular religion is now hung on a metaphysical hypothesis, which itself has been in vogue for only a few centuries in the history of speculation, and which is now become to those trained in positive habits of thought a mere juggle of ideas.

We have in all this sought only to state what we mean by man's soul, and what we do not mean. But we make no attempt to prove a negative, or to demonstrate the non-existence of the supposed entity. Our purpose now is a very different one. We start out from this—that this positive mode of treating man is in this, as in other things, morally sufficient; that it leaves no voids and chasms in human life ; that the moral and religious sequelæ which are sometimes assigned to its teaching have no foundation in fact. We say that, on this basis, not only have we an entrance into the spiritual realm, but that we have a firmer hold on the spiritual life than on the basis of hypothesis. On this theory, the world beyond the grave is in closer and truer relation to conduct than on the spiritualist theory. We look on man as man, not as man *plus* a heterogeneous entity. And we think that we lose nothing, but gain much thereby, in the religious as well as in the moral world. We do not deny the conceivable existence of the heterogeneous entity. But we believe that human nature is adequately equipped on human and natural grounds without this disparate nondescript.

Let us be careful to describe the method we employ as that which looks on man as man, and repudiate the various labels, such as materialists, physical, unspiritual methods, and the like, which are used as equivalent for the rational or positive method of treating man. The method of treating man as man insists, at least as much as any other method, that man has a moral, emotional, religious life, different in kind from his material and practical life, but perfectly coördinate with that physical life, and to be studied on similar scientific methods. The spiritual sympathies of man are undoubtedly the highest part of human nature; and our method condemns as loudly as any system physical explanations of spiritual life. We claim the right to use the term "soul," "spiritual," and the like, in their natural meaning. In the same way, we think that there are theories which are justly called "materialist," that there are physical conceptions of human nature which are truly dangerous to morality, to goodness, and religion. It is sometimes thought to be a sufficient proof of the reality of this heterogeneous entity of the soul, that otherwise we must assume the most spiritual emotions of man to be a secretion of cerebral matter, and that, whatever the difficulties of conceiving the union of soul and body, it is something less difficult than the conceiving that the nerves think, or the tissues love. We repudiate such

language as much as any one can, but there is
another alternative. It is possible to invest with
the highest dignity the spiritual life of mankind by
treating it as an ultimate fact, without trying to find
an explanation for it either in a perfectly unthinkable
hypothesis or in an irrational and debasing physicism.

 We certainly do reject, as earnestly as any school can,
that which is most fairly called materialism, and we will
second every word of those who cry out that civilization is,
in danger if the workings of the human spirit are to become
questions of physiology, and if death is the end of a man,
as it is the end of a sparrow. We not only assent to such
protests, but we see very pressing need for making them.
It is a corrupting doctrine to open a brain, and to tell us that
devotion is a definite molecular change in this and that
convolution of gray pulp, and that if man is the first of
living animals, he passes away after a short space like the
beasts that perish. And all doctrines, more or less, do tend
to this, which offer physical theories as explaining moral
phenomena, which deny man a spiritual in addition to a
moral nature, which limit his moral life to the span of his
bodily organism, and which have no place for " religion "
in the proper sense of the word.

It is true that in this age, or rather in this country, we
seldom hear the stupid and brutal materialism which pretends that subtilties of thought and emotion are simply
this or that agitation in some gray matter, to be ultimately expounded by the professors of gray matter. But
this is hardly the danger which besets our time. The true

materialism to fear is the prevailing tendency of anatomical habits of mind or specialist habits of mind to intrude into the regions of religion and philosophy. A man whose whole thoughts are absorbed in cutting up dead monkeys and live frogs has no more business to dogmatize about religion than a mere chemist to improvise a zoölogy. Biological reasoning about spiritual things is as presumptuous as the theories of an electrician about the organic facts of nervous life. We live amid a constant and growing usurpation of science in the province of philosophy; of biology in the province of sociology; of physics in that of religion. Nothing is more common than the use of the term science, when what is meant is merely physical and physiological science, not social and moral science. The arrogant attempt to dispose of the deepest moral truths of human nature on a bare physical or physiological basis is almost enough to justify the insurrection of some impatient theologians against science itself. It is impossible not to sympathize with men who at least are defending the paramount claim of the moral laws and the religious sentiment. The solution of the dispute is, of course, that physicists and theologians have each hold of a partial truth. As the latter insist, the grand problem of man's life must be ever referred to moral and social argument; but then, as the physicist insists, this moral and social argument can only be built up on a physical and physiological foundation. The physical part of science is, indeed, merely the vestibule to social, and thence to moral science; and of science in all its forms the philosophy of religion alone holds the key.

The true materialism lies in the habit of scientific specialists to neglect all philosophical and religious synthesis. It is marked by the ignoring of religion, the passing by on the other side, and shutting the eyes to the spiritual history of mankind. The spiritual traditions of mankind, a supreme philosophy of life and thought, religion in the proper sense of the word, all these have to play a larger and ever larger part in human knowledge; not as we are so often told, and so commonly is assumed, a waning and vanishing part. And it is in this field, the field which has so long been abandoned to theology, that Positivism is prepared to meet the theologians. We at any rate do not ask them to submit religion to the test of the scalpel or the electric battery. It is true that we base our theory of society and our theory of morals, and hence our religion itself, on a curriculum of physical and especially of biological science. It is true that our moral and social science is but a prolongation of these other sciences. But, then, we insist that it is not science in the narrow sense which can order our beliefs, but philosophy; not science which can solve our problems of life, but religion. And religion demands for its understanding the religious mind and the spiritual experience.

Does it seem to any one a paradox to hold such language, and yet to have nothing to say about the immaterial entity which may assume to be the *cause* behind this spiritual life? The answer is, that we occupy ourselves with this spiritual life as an ultimate fact; and, consistently with the whole of our philosophy, we decline to assign a

3

cause at all. We argue, with the theologians, that it is ridiculous to go to the scalpel for an adequate account of a mother's love ; but we do not think it is explained (any more than it is by the scalpel) by an hypothesis for which not only is there no shadow of evidence, but which cannot even be stated in philosophic language. We find the same absurdity in the notion that maternal love is a branch of the anatomy of the *mammæ*, and in the notion that the phenomena of lactation are produced by an immaterial entity. Both are forms of the same fallacy, that of trying to reach ultimate causes instead of studying laws. We certainly do find that maternal love and lactation have close correspondences, and that both are phenomena of certain female organisms. And we say that to talk of maternal love being exhibited by an entity which not only is not a female organism, but is not an organism at all, is to use language which to us, at least, is unintelligible.

The philosophy which treats man as man simply affirms that *man* loves, thinks, acts, not that the ganglia, or the sinuses, or any organ of man, loves and thinks and acts. The thoughts, aspirations, and impulses, are not secretions, and the science which teaches us about secretions will not teach us much about them ; our thoughts, aspirations, and impulses, are faculties of a man. Now, as a man implies a body, so we say these also imply a body. And to talk to us about a bodiless being thinking and loving is simply to talk about the thoughts and feelings of nothing.

This fundamental position each one determines according to the whole bias of his intellectual and moral nature·

But on the positive, as on the theological, method there is ample scope for the spiritual life, for moral responsibility, for the world beyond the grave, its hopes and its duties; which remain to us perfectly real without the unintelligible hypothesis. However much men cling to the hypothesis from old association, if they reflect, they will find that they do not use it to give them any actual knowledge about man's spiritual life; that all their methodical reasoning about the moral world is exclusively based on the phenomena of this world, and not on the phenomena of any other world. And thus the absence of the hypothesis altogether does not make the serious difference which theolologians suppose.

To follow out this into particulars : Analysis of human nature shows us man with a great variety of faculties; his moral powers are just as distinguishable as his intellectual powers ; and both are mentally separable from his physical powers. Moral and mental laws are reduced to something like system by moral and mental science, with or without the theological hypothesis. The most extreme form of materialism does not dispute that moral and mental science is for logical purposes something more than physical science. So the most extreme form of spiritualism gets its mental and moral science by observation and argument from phenomena ; it does not, or it does not any longer, build such science by abstract deduction from any proposition as to an immaterial entity. There have been, in ages past, attempts to do this. Plato, for instance, attempted to found, not only his mental and moral philosophy, but his general philosophy of the universe, by deduction from a mere hypothesis. He imagined immaterial entities, the ideas of things inorganic, as much as organic. But then Plato was consistent and had the courage of his opinions. If he imagined an idea, or soul, of a man, he imagined one also for a dog, for a tree, for a statue, for a chair. He thought that a statue and a chair were what they are, by virtue of an immaterial entity which gave them form. The hypothesis did not add much to the art of statuary, or to that of the carpenter; nor to do him justice, did Plato look for much practical result in these spheres. One form of the doctrine alone survives —that man is what he is by virtue of an immaterial entity temporally indwelling in his body. But, though the hypothesis survives, it is in no sense any longer the basis of the science of human nature with any school. No school is now content to sit in its study and evolve its knowledge of the moral qualities of man out of abstract deductions from the conception of an immaterial entity. All, without exception, profess to get their knowledge of the moral qualities by observing the qualities which men actually do exhibit, or have exhibited. And those who are persuaded that man has, over and above his man's nature, an immaterial entity, find themselves discussing the laws of thought and of character on a common ground with those who regard man as man—i. e., who regard man's nature as capable of being referred to an homogeneous system of law. Spiritualists and materialists, however much they may differ in their explanations of moral phenomena, describe their relations in the same language, the language of law, not of illuminism.

Those, therefore, who dispense with a transcendental explanation are just as free as those who maintain it, to handle the spiritual and religious phenomena of human nature, treating them simply as phenomena. No one has ever suggested that the former philosophy is not quite as well entitled to analyze the intellectual faculties of man, as the stoutest believer in the immaterial entity. It would raise a smile now-a-days to hear it said that such a one must be incompetent to treat of the canons of inductive reasoning, because he was unorthodox as to the immortality of the soul. And if, notwithstanding this unorthodoxy, he is thought competent to investigate the laws of thought, why not the moral laws, the sentiments, and the emotions? As a fact, every moral faculty of man is recognized by him just as much as by any transcendentalist. He does not limit himself, any more than the theologian does, to mere morality. He is fully alive to the spiritual emotions in all their depth, purity, and beauty. He recognizes in man the yearning for a power outside his individual self, which he may venerate, a love for the author of his chief good, the need for sympathy with something greater than himself. All these are positive facts which rest on observation, quite apart from any explanation of the hypothetical cause of these tendencies in man. There, at any rate, the scientific observer finds them; and he is at liberty to give them quite as high a place in his scheme of human nature as the most complete theologian. He may possibly give them a far higher place, and bind them far more truly into the entire tissue of his whole view of life, because they are built up for him on precisely the same ground of experience as all the rest of his knowledge, and have no element at all heterogeneous from the rest of life. With the language of spiritual emotion he is perfectly in unison. The spirit of devotion, of spiritual communion with an ever-present power, of sympathy and fellowship with the living world, of awe and submission toward the material world, the sense of adoration, love, resignation, mystery, are at least as potent with the one system as with the other. He can share the religious emotion of every age, and can enter into the language of every truly religious heart. For myself, I believe that this is only done on a complete as well as a real basis in the religion of humanity, but we need not confine the present argument to that ground. I venture to believe that this spirit is truly shared by all, whatever their hypothesis about the human soul, who treat these highest emotions of man's nature as facts of primary value, and who have any intelligible theory whereby these emotions can be aroused.

All positive methods of treating man of a comprehensive kind, adopt to the full all that has ever been said about the dignity of man's moral and spiritual life, and treat these phenomena as distinct from the intellectual and the physical life. These methods also recognize the unity of consciousness, the facts of conscience, the sense of identity, and the longing for perpetuation of that identity. They decline to explain these phenomena by the popular hypotheses; but they neither deny their existence nor lessen their importance. Man, they argue, has a complex existence, made up of the phenomena of his physical organs, of his intellectual powers, of his moral faculties, crowned and harmonized ultimately by his religious sympathies—love, gratitude, veneration, submission, toward the dominant force by which he finds himself surrounded. I use words which are not limited to a particular philosophy or religion—I do not now confine my language to the philosophy or religion of Comte—for this same conception of man is common to many philosophies and many religions. It characterizes such systems as those of Spinoza or Shelley or Fichte as much as those of Confucius or Buddha. In a word, the reality and the supremacy of the spiritual life have never been carried further than by men who have departed most widely from the popular hypotheses of the immaterial entity.

Many of these men, no doubt, have indulged in hypotheses of their own, quite as arbitrary as those of theology. It is characteristic of the positive thought of our age that it stands upon a firmer basis. Though not confounding the moral facts with the physical, it will never lose sight of the correspondence and consensus between all sides of human life. Led by an enormous and complete array of evidence, it associates every fact of thought or of emotion with a fact of physiology, with molecular change in the body. Without pretending to explain the first by the second, it denies that the first can be explained without the second. But with this solid basis of reality to work on, it gives their place of supremacy to the highest sensibilities of man, through the heights and depths of the spiritual life.

Nothing is more idle than a discussion about words. But when some deny the use of the word " soul " to those who mean by it this consensus, and not any immaterial entity, we may remind them that our use of the word agrees with its etymology and its history. It is the mode in which it is used in the Bible, the well-spring of our true English speech. It may, indeed, be contended that there is no instance in the Bible in which soul does mean an immaterial entity, the idea not having been familiar to any of the writers, with the doubtful exception of St. Paul. But without entering upon Biblical philology, it may be said that for one passage in the Bible in which the word "soul" can be forced to bear the meaning of immaterial entity, there are ten texts in which it cannot possibly refer to anything but breath, life, moral sense, or spiritual emotion. When the Psalmist says, " Deliver my soul from death," "Heal my soul, for I have sinned," "My soul is cast down within me," "Return unto my rest, O my soul," he means by " soul " what we mean—the conscious unity of our being culminating in its religious emotions ; and until we find some English word that better expresses this idea, we shall continue to use the phraseology of David.

It is not merely that we are denied the language of religion, but we sometimes find attempts to exclude us from the thing. There are some who say that worship, spiritual life, and that exaltation of the sentiments which we call devotion, have no possible meaning unless applied to the special theology of the particular speaker. A little attention to history, a single reflection on religion as a whole, suffice to show the hollowness of this assumption. If devotion mean the surrender of self to an adored Power, there has been devotion in creeds with many gods, with one God, with no gods; if spiritual life mean the cultivation of this temper toward moral purification, there was spiritual life long before the notion of an immaterial entity inside the human being was excogitated; and as to worship, men have worshipped, with intense and overwhelming passion, all kinds of objects,—organic and inorganic, material and spiritual, abstract ideas as well as visible forces. Is it implied that Confucius, and the countless millions who have followed him, had no idea of religion, as it is certain that they had none of theology; that Buddha and the Buddhists were incapable of spiritual emotion; that the Fire-worshippers and the Sun-worshippers never practised worship; that the pantheists and the humanists, from Marcus Aurelius to Fichte, had the springs of spiritual life dried up in them for want of an Old or New Testament? If this is intended, one can only wonder at the power of a self-complacent conformity to close men's eyes to the native dignity of man. Religion, and its elements in emotion—attachment, veneration, love,—are as old exactly as human nature. They moved the first men and the first women; they have found a hundred objects to inspire them, and have bowed to a great variety of powers. They were in full force long before theology was, and before the rise of Christianity; and it would be strange indeed if it should cease with the decline of either. It is not the emotional elements of religion which fail us; for these, with the growing goodness of mankind, are gaining in purity and strength. Rather it is the intellectual elements of religion which are conspicuously at fault. We need to-day, not the faculty of worship (that is ever fresh in the heart), but a clearer vision of the power we should worship. Nay, it is not we who are borrowing the privileges of theology: rather it is theology which seeks to appropriate to itself the most universal privilege of man.

II.

THE rational view of the soul (we insisted in a previous paper) would remove us as far from cynical materialism as from a fantastic spiritualism. It restores to their true supremacy in human life those religious emotions which materialism forgets; while it frees us from the idle figment which spiritualism would foist upon human nature.

We entirely agree with the theologians that our age is beset with a grievous danger of materialism. There is a school of teachers abroad, and they have found an echo here, who dream that victorious vivisection will ultimately win them anatomical solutions of man's moral and spiritual mysteries. Such unholy nightmares, it is true, are not likely to beguile many minds in a country like this, where social and moral problems are still in their natural ascendant. But there is a subtiler kind of materialism, of which the dangers are real. It does not, indeed, put forth the bestial sophism that the apex of philosophy is to be won by improved microscopes and new batteries. But, then, it has nothing to say about the spiritual life of man; it has no particular religion; it ignores the soul. It fills the air with pæans to science; it is never weary of vaunting the scientific methods, the scientific triumphs. But it always means physical, not moral science; intellectual, not religious conquests. It shirks the question of questions—to what human end is this knowledge?—how shall man thereby order his life as a whole?—where is he to find the object of his yearnings of spirit? Of the spiritual history of mankind it knows as little, and thinks as little, as of any other sort of Asiatic devil-worship. At the spiritual aspirations of the men and women around us, ill at ease for want of some answer, it stares blankly, as it does at some spirit-rapping epidemic. "What is that to us?—see thou to that"—is all that it can answer when men ask it for a religion. It is of the religion of all sensible men, the religion which all sensible men never tell. With a smile or a shrug of the shoulders it passes by into the whirring workshops of science (that is, the physical prelude of science); and it leaves the spiritual life of the soul to the spiritualists, theological or nonsensical as the case may be, wishing them both in heaven. This is the materialism to fear.

The theologians and the vast sober mass of serious men and women, who want simply to live rightly, are quite right when they shun and fear a school that is so eager about cosmology and biology, while it leaves morality and religion to take care of themselves. And yet they know all the while that before the advancing line of positive thought they are fighting a forlorn hope; and they see their own line daily more and more demoralized by the consciousness that they have no rational plan of campaign. They know that their own account of the soul, of the spiritual life, of Providence, of heaven, is daily shifting—is growing more vague, more inconsistent, more various. They hurry wildly from one untenable position to another, like a routed and disorganized army. In a religious discussion years ago we once asked one of the Broad Church, · a disciple of one of its eminent founders, what he understood by the Third Person of the Trinity; and he said, doubtfully, that "he fancied there was a sort of a something." Since those days the process of disintegration and vaporization of belief has gone on rapidly; and now very religious minds, and men who think themselves to be religious, are ready to apply this "sort of a something" to all the verities in turn. They half hope that there is "a sort of something" fluttering about, or inside, their human frames, that there may turn out to be a "something" somewhere after death, and that there must be a sort of a somebody or (as the theology of culture will have it) a sort of a something controlling and and comprehending human life. But the more thoughtful spirits, not being professionally engaged in a doctrine, mostly limit themselves to a pious hope that there may be something in it, and that we shall know some day what it is.

Now, theologians and religious people unattached must know that this will never serve—that this is paltering with the greatest of all things. What, then, is the only solution which can ultimately satisfy both the devotees of science and the believers in religion? Surely but this, to make religion scientific by placing religion under the methods of science. Let science come to see that religion, morality, life, are within its field, or, rather, are the main part of its field. Let religion come to see that it can be nothing but a prolongation of science, a rational and homogeneous result of cosmology and biology, not a matter of fantastic guessing. Then there will be no true science which does not aim at, and is not guided by, systematic religion. And there will be no religion which pretends to any other basis but positive knowledge and scientific logic. But for this science must consent to add spiritual phenomena to its curriculum, and religion must consent to give up its vapid figments.

Positivism in dealing with the soul discards the exploded errors of the materialists and spiritualists alike. On the one hand, it not only admits into its studies the spiritual life of men, but it raises this life to be the essential business of all human knowledge. All the spiritual sentiments of man, the aspirations of the conscious soul in all their purity and pathos, the vast religious experience and potentialities of the human heart seen in the history of our spiritual life as a race—this is, we say, the principal subject of science and of philosophy. No philosophy, no morality, no polity, can rest on stable foundations if this be not its grand aim ; if it have not a systematic creed, a rational object of worship, and a definite discipline of life. But, then, we treat these spiritual functions of the soul, not as mystical enigmas, but as positive phenomena, and we satisfy them by philosophic and historic answers and not by naked figments. And we think that the teaching of history and a true synthesis of science bring us far closer to the heart of this spiritual life than do any spiritualist guesses, and do better equip us to read aright the higher secrets of the soul : meaning always by soul the consensus of the faculties which observation discovers in the human organism.

On the other hand, without entering into an idle dispute with the spiritualist orthodoxy, we insist on regarding this organism as a perfectly homogeneous unit, to be studied from one end of it to the other by rational scientific methods. We pretend to give no sort of *cause* as lying behind the manifold powers of the organism. We say the immaterial entity is something which we cannot grasp, which explains nothing, for which we cannot have a shadow of evidence. We are determined to treat man as a human organism, just as we treat a dog as a canine organism ; and we know no ground for saying, and no good to be got by pretending, that man is a human organism *plus* an indescribable entity. We say the human organism is a marvellous thing, sublime if you will, of subtilest faculty and sensibility; but we, at any rate, can find nothing in man which is not an organic part of this organism; we find the faculties of mind, feeling, and will, directly dependent on physical organs; and to talk to us of mind, feeling, and will, continuing their functions in the absence of physical organs and visible organisms, is to use language which, to us at least, is pure nonsense.

And now to turn to the grand phenomenon of material organisms which we call Death. The human organism, like every other organism, ultimately loses that unstable equilibrium of its correlated forces which we name Life, and ceases to be an organism or system of organs, adjusting its internal relations to its external conditions. Thereupon the existence of the complex independent entity to which we attribute consciousness undoubtedly—i. e., for aught we know to the contrary—comes to an end. But the activities of this organism do not come to an end, except so far as these activities need fresh sensations and material organs. And a great part of these activities, and far the noblest part, only need fresh sensations and material organs in other similar organisms. While there is an abundance of these in due relation, the activities go on *ad infinitum*, with increasing energy. We have not the slightest reason to suppose that the consciousness of the organism continues, for we mean by consciousness the sum of sensations of a particular organism, and the particular organism being dissolved, we have nothing left whereto to attribute consciousness, and the proposal strikes us like a proposal to regard infinity as conscious. So, of course, with the sensations separately, and with them the power of accumulating knowledge, of feeling, thinking, or of modifying the existence in correspondence with the outward environment. Life, in the technical sense of the word, is at an end, but the activities of which that life is the source were never so potent. Our age is familiar enough with the truth of the persistence of energy, and no one supposes that with the dissolution of the body the forces of its material elements are lost. They only pass into new combinations and continue to work elsewhere. Far less is the energy of the activities lost. The earth, and every country, every farmstead, and every city on it, are standing witnesses that the physical activities are not lost. As century rolls after century, we see in every age more potent fruits of the labour which raised the pyramids, or won Holland from the sea, or carved the Theseus out of marble. The bodily organisms which wrought them have passed into gases and earths, but the activity they displayed is producing the precise results designed on a far grander scale in each generation. Much more do the intellectual and moral energies work unceasingly. Not a single manifestation of thought or feeling is without some result so soon as it is communicated to a similar organism. It passes into the sum of his mental and moral being.

But there is about the persistence of the moral energies this special phenomenon. It marks the vast interval between physical and moral science. The energies of ma-

terial elements, so far as we see, disperse, or for the most
part disperse. The energies of an intellectual and moral
kind are very largely continued in their organic unities.
The consensus of the mental, of the moral, of the emotional powers may go on, working as a whole, producing
precisely the same results, with the same individuality,
whether the material organism, the source and original
base of these.powers, be in physical function or not. The
mental and moral powers do not, it is true, increase and
grow, develop or vary, within themselves. Nor do they
in their special individuality produce visible results, for
they are no longer in direct relations with their special
material organisms. But the mental and moral powers
are not dispersed like gases. They retain their unity,
they retain their organic character, and they retain the
whole of their power of passing into and stimulating the
brains of living men ; and in these they carry on their
activity precisely as they did, while the bodies in which
they were formed absorbed and exhaled material substance.

Nay, more : the individuality and true activity of these
mental and moral forces is often not manifest, and sometimes is not complete, so long as the organism continues
its physical functions. Newton, we may suppose, has accomplished his great researches. They are destined to
transform half the philosophy of mankind. But he is
old, and incapable of fresh achievements. We will say
he is feeble, secluded, silent, and lives shut up in his
rooms. The activity of his mighty intellectual nature is

4

being borne over the world on the wings of Thought, and works a revolution at every stroke. But otherwise the man Newton is not essentially distinguishable from the nearest infirm pauper, and has as few and as feeble relations with mankind. At last the man Newton dies—that is, the body is dispersed into gas and dust. But the world, which is affected enormously by his intellect, is not in the smallest degree affected by his death.. His activity continues the same ; if it were worth while to conceal the fact of his death, no one of the millions who are so greatly affected by his thoughts would perceive it or know it. If he had discovered some means of prolonging a torpid existence till this hour, he might be living now, and it would not signify to us in the slightest degree whether his body breathed in the walls of his lodgings or mouldered in the vaults of the Abbey.

It may be said that, if it does not signify much to us, it signifies a great deal to Isaac Newton. But is this true ? He no longer eats and sleeps, a burden to himself; he no longer is destroying his great name by feeble theology or querulous pettiness. But if the small weaknesses and wants of the flesh are ended for him, all that makes Newton (and he had always lived for his posthumous, not his immediate, fame) rises into greater activity and purer uses. We make no mystical or fanciful divinity of Death ; we do not deny its terrors or its evils. We are not responsible for it, and should welcome any reasonable prospect of eliminating or postponing this fatality, that waits upon all organic Nature. But it is no answer to philosophy or science to retort that Death is so terrible, therefore man must be designed to escape it. There are savages who persistently deny that men do die at all, either their bodies or their souls, asserting that the visible consequences of death are either an illusion or an artfully-contrived piece of acting on the part of their friends, who have really decamped to the happy hunting-fields. This seems on the whole a more rational theory than that of immaterial souls flying about space, as the spontaneous fancies of savages are sometimes more rational than the elaborate hypotheses of metaphysics.

But though we do not presume to apologize for death, it is easy to see that many of the greatest moral and intellectual results of life are only possible, can only begin, when the claims of the animal life are satisfied; when the stormy, complex, and checkered career is over, and the higher tops of the intellectual or moral nature alone stand forth in the distance of time. What was the blind old harper of Scio to his contemporaries, or the querulous refugee from Florence, or even the boon-companion and retired playwright of Stratford, or the blind and stern old malignant of Bunhill Field? The true work of Socrates and his life only began with his resplendent death, to say nothing of yet greater religious teachers, whose names I refrain from citing; and as to those whose lives have been cast in conflicts—the Cæsars, the Alfreds, the Hildebrands, the Cromwells, the Fredericks—it is only after death, oftenest in ages after death, that they cease to be com batants, and become creators. It is not merely that they

are only recognized in after ages ; the truth is, that their
activity only begins when the surging of passion and sense
ends, and turmoil dies away.   Great intellects and great
characters are necessarily in advance of their age; the
care of the father and the mother begins to tell most
truly in the ripe manhood of their children, when the
parents are often in the grave, and not in the infancy
which they see and are confronted with.   The great must
always feel with Kepler, " It is enough, as yet, if I have
a hearer now and then in a century." John Brown's body
lies a-mouldering in the grave, but his soul is marching
along.

We can trace this truth best in the case of great men ;
but it is not confined to the great.   Not a single act of
thought or character ends with itself.   Nay more ; not a
single nature in its entirety but leaves its influence for
good or for evil.   As a fact the good prevail ; but all act,
all continue to act indefinitely, often in ever-widening
circles.   Physicists amuse us by tracing for us the infinite
fortunes of some wave set in motion by force, its circles
and its repercussions perpetually transmitted in new com-
plications. But the career of a single intellect and character is a far more real force when it meets with suitable
intellects and characters into whose action it is incorporated.   Every life more or less forms another life, and
lives in another life.   Civilization, nation, city, imply this
fact.   There is neither mysticism nor hyperbole, but simple observation in the belief, that the career of every human being in society does not end with the death of its

body. In some sort its higher activities and potency can only begin truly when change is no longer possible for it. The worthy gain in influence and in range at each generation, just as the founders of some populous race gain a greater fatherhood at each succeeding growth of their descendants. And, in some infinitesimal degree, the humblest life that ever turned a sod sends a wave—no, more than a wave, a life—through the ever-growing harmony of human society. Not a soldier died at Marathon or Salamis, but did a stroke by which our thought is enlarged and our standard of duty formed to this day.

Be it remembered that this is not hypothesis, but something perfectly real—we may fairly say undeniable. We are not inventing an imaginary world, and saying it must be real because it is so pleasant to think of ; we are only repeating truths on which our notion of history and society is based. The idea, no doubt, is usually limited to the famous, and to the great revolutions in civilization. But no one who thinks it out carefully can deny that it is true of every human being in society in some lesser degree. The idea has not been, or is no longer, systematically enforced, invested with poetry and dignity, and deepened by the solemnity of religion. But why is that? Because theological hypotheses of a new and heterogeneous existence have deadened our interest in the realities, the grandeur, and the perpetuity of our earthly life. In the best days of Rome, even without a theory of history or a science of society, it was a living faith, the true religion of that majestic race. It is the real sentiment of all societies where the theological hypothesis has disappeared. It is no doubt now in England the great motive of virtue and energy. There have been few seasons in the world's history when the sense of moral responsibility and moral survival after death was more exalted and more vigorous than with the companions of Vergniaud and Danton, to whom the dreams of theology were hardly intelligible. As we read the calm and humane words of Condorcet on the very edge of his yawning grave, we learn how the conviction of posthumous activity (not of posthumous fame), how the consciousness of a coming incorporation with the glorious future of his race, can give a patience and a happiness equal to that of any martyr of theology.

It would be an endless inquiry to trace the means whereby this sense of posthumous participation in the life of our fellows can be extended to the mass, as it certainly affects already the thoughtful and the refined. Without an education, a new social opinion, without a religion—I mean an organized religion, not a vague metaphysic—it is doubtless impossible that it should become universal and capable of overcoming selfishness. But make it at once the basis of philosophy, the standard of right and wrong, and the centre of a religion, and this will prove, perhaps, an easier task than that of teaching Greeks and Romans, Syrians and Moors, to look forward to a future life of ceaseless psalmody in an immaterial heaven. The astonishing feat was performed; and, perhaps, it may be easier to fashion a new public opinion, requiring merely that an accepted truth of philosophy should be popularized, which is already the deepest hope of some thoughtful spirits and which does not take the suicidal course of trying to cast out the devil of selfishness by a direct appeal to the personal self.

It is here that the strength of the human future over the celestial future is so clearly pre-eminent. Make the future hope a social activity, and we give to the present life a social ideal. Make the future hope personal beatitude, and personality is stamped deeper on every act of of our daily life. Now we make the future hope, in the truest sense, social, inasmuch as our future is simply an active existence prolonged by society. And our future hope rests not in any vague yearning, of which we have as little evidence as we have definite conception : it rests on a perfectly certain truth, accepted by all thoughtful minds, the truth that the actions, feelings, thoughts, of every one of us—our minds, our characters, our *souls*, as organic wholes—do marvellously influence and mould each other; that the highest part of ourselves, the abiding part of us, passes into other lives and continues to live in other lives. Can we conceive a more potent stimulus to rectitude, to daily and hourly striving after true life, than this ever-present sense that we are indeed immortal ; not that we have an immortal something within us, but that in very truth we ourselves, our thinking, feeling, acting personalities, are immortal; nay, cannot die, but must ever continue what we make them, working and doing, if no longer receiving and enjoying ? And not merely we ourselves, in our personal identity, are immortal, but each act, thought, and feeling, is immortal ; and this immortality is not some ecstatic and indescribable condition in space, but activity on earth in the real and known work of life, in the welfare of those whom we have loved, and in the happiness of those who come after us.

And can it be difficult to idealize and give currency to a faith which is a certain and undisputed fact of common sense as well as of philosophy ? As we *live for others* in life, so we *live in others* after death, as others have lived in us, and all for the common race. How deeply does such a belief as this bring home to each moment of life the mysterious perpetuity of ourselves! For good, for evil, we cannot die ; we cannot shake ourselves free from this eternity of our faculties. There is here no promise, it is true, of eternal sensations, enjoyments, meditations. There is no promise, be it plainly said, of anything but an immortality of influence, of spiritual work, of glorified activity. We cannot even say that we shall continue to love ; but we know that we shall be loved. It may well be that we shall consciously know no hope ourselves ; but we shall inspire hopes. It may be that we shall not think ; but others will think our thoughts, and enshrine our minds. If no sympathies shall thrill along our nerves, we shall be the spring of sympathy in distant generations ; and that, though we be the humblest and the least of all the soldiers in the human host, the least celebrated and the worst remembered. For our lives live when we are most forgotten ; and not a cup of water that we may have given to an unknown sufferer, or a wise word spoken in season to a child, but has added (whether we remember it, whether others remember it or not) a streak of happiness and strength to the world. Our earthly frames, like the grain of wheat, may be laid in the earth—and this image of our great spiritual Master is more fit for the social than for the celestial future—but the grain shall bear spiritual fruit, and multiply in kindred natures and in other selves.

It is a merely verbal question if this be the life of the Soul when the Soul means the sum of the activities, or if there be any immortality where there is no consciousness. It is enough for us that we can trust to a real prolongation of our highest activity in the sensible lives of others, even though our own forces can gain nothing new, and are not reflected in a sensitive body. We do not get rid of Death, but we transfigure Death. Does any religion profess to do more ? It is enough for any creed that it can teach *non omnis moriar ;* it would be gross extravagance to say *omnis non moriar,* no part of me shall die. Death is the one inevitable law of Life. The business of religion is to show us what are its compensations. The spiritualist orthodoxy, like every other creed, is willing to allow that Death robs us of a great deal, that very much of us does die ; nay, it teaches that this dies utterly, forever, leaving no trace but dust. And thus the spiritualist orthodoxy exaggerates death, and adds a fresh terror to its power. We, on the contrary, would seek to show that much of us, and that the best of us, does not die, or at least does not end. And the difference between our faith and that of

the orthodox is this : we look to the permanence of the
activities which give others happiness ; they look to the
permanence of the consciousness which can enjoy happiness.   Which is the nobler ?

What need we then to promise or to hope more than an
eternity of spiritual influence ?   Yet, after all, 'tis no
question as to what kind of eternity man would prefer to
select.   We have no evidence that he has any choice before him.   If we are creating a universe of our own and
a human race on an ideal mould, it might be rational to
discuss what kind of eternity was the most desirable, and
it might then become a question if we should not begin by
eliminating death.   But as we are, with death in the world,
and man as we know him submitting to the fatality of his
nature, the rational inquiry is this—how best to order his
life, and to use the eternity that he has.   And an immortality of prolonged activity on earth he has as certainly
as he has civilization, or progress, or society.   And the wise
man in the evening of life may be well content to say :
" I have worked and thought, and have been conscious in
the flesh ; I have done with the flesh, and therewith with
the toil of thought and the troubles of sensation ; I am
ready to pass into the spiritual community of human
souls, and when this man's flesh wastes away from me,
may I be found worthy to become part of the influence of
humanity itself, and so

> ' .   .   .   .   join the choir invisible
> Whose music is the gladness of the world.' "

That the doctrine of the celestial future appeals to the

essence of self appears very strongly in its special rebuke
to the doctrine of the social future. It repeats: "We
agree with all you say about the prolonged activity of
man after death, we see of course that the solid achievements of life are carried on, and we grant you that it signifies nothing to those who profit by his work that the
man no longer breathes in the flesh ; but what is all that
to the *man*, to you, and to me ? We shall not *feel* our
work ; we shall not have the indescribable satisfaction
which our souls now have in living, in effecting our work,
and profiting by others. What is the good of mankind
to me, when I am mouldering unconscious ?" This is the
true materialism ; here is the physical theory of another
life ; this is the unspiritual denial of the soul, the binding
it down to the clay of the body. We say, " All that is
great in you shall not end, but carry on its activity perpetually and in a purer way ; " and you reply : " What
care I for what is great in me, and its possible work in this
vale of tears ? I want to feel life, I want to enjoy, I want
my personality"—in other words, " I want my senses, I
want my body." Keep your body and keep your senses
in any way that you know. We can only wonder
and say, with Frederick to his runaway soldiers, "Wollt
ihr immer leben ? " But we, who know that a higher
form of activity is only to be reached by a subjective life
in society, will continue to regard a perpetuity of sensation
as the true hell, for we feel that the perpetual worth of our
lives is the one thing precious to care for, and not a vacu-
ous eternity of consciousness,

It is not merely that this eternity of the tabor is so gross, so sensual, so indolent, so selfish a creed; but its worst evil is that it paralyzes practical life, and throws it into discord. A life of vanity in a vale of tears to be followed by an infinity of celestial rapture, is necessarily a life which is of infinitesimal importance. The incongruity of the attempts to connect the two, and to make the vale of tears the antechamber of the judgment-dock of heaven, grows greater and not less as ages roll on. The more we think and learn, and the higher rises our social philosophy and our insight into human destiny, the more the reality and importance of the social future impresses us, while the fancy of the celestial future grows unreal and incongruous. As we get to know what thinking means, and feeling means, and the more truly we understand what life means, the more completely do the promises of the celestial transcendentalism fail to interest us. We have come to see that to continue to live is to carry on a series of correlated sensations, and to set in motion a series of corresponding forces ; to think is to marshal a set of observed perceptions with a view to certain observed phenomena to feel implies something of which we have a real assurance affecting our own consensus within. The whole set of positive thoughts compels us to believe that it is an infinite apathy to which your heaven would consign us, without objects, without relations, without change, without growth, without action, an absolute nothingness, a *nirvana* of impotence—this is not life; it is not consciousness ; it is not happiness. So far as we can grasp the hypothesis, it seems equally ludicrous and repulsive. You may call it paradise; but we call it conscious annihilation. You may long for it, if you have been so taught; just as if you had been taught to cherish such hopes, you might be now yearning for the moment when you might become the immaterial principle of a comet, or as you might tell me that you really were the ether, and were about to take your place in space. This is how these sublimities affect us. But we know that to many this future is one of spiritual development, a life of growth and continual up-soaring of still higher affection. It may be so; but to our mind these are contradictions in terms. We cannot understand what life and affection can mean, where you postulate the absence of every condition by which life and affection are possible. Can there be development where there is no law, thought or affection where object and subject are confused into one essence? How can that be existence, where everything of which we have experience, and everything which we can define, is presumed to be unable to enter? To us these things are all incoherences; and in the midst of practical realities and the solid duties of life, sheer impertinences. The field is full: each human life has a perfectly real and a vast future to look torward to; these hyperbolic enigmas disturb our grave duties and our solid hopes. No wonder, then, while they are still so rife, that men are dull to the moral responsibility which, in its awfulness, begins only at the grave; that they are so little influenced by the futurity which will judge them; that they are blind to the dignity and beauty of death, and shuffle off the dead life and the dead body with such cruel disrespect. The fumes of the celestial immortality still confuse them. It is only when an earthly future is the fulfilment of a worthy, earthly life, that we can see all the majesty as well as the glory of the world beyond the grave ; and then only will it fulfil its moral and religious purpose as the great guide of human conduct.

————

R. H. HUTTON.

THE imaginative glow and rhetorical vivacity which are visible throughout Mr. Harrison's essays on "The Soul and Future Life" are very remarkable, and should guard those of us who recoil in amazement from its creed or no-creed from falling into the very common mistake of assuming that the effect which such ideas as these produce on ourselves is *the* effect, which, apart from all questions of the other mental conditions surrounding the natures into which they are received, they naturally produce. It is clear, at least, that if they ever tended to produce on the author of these papers the same effect which they not only tend to produce, but do produce on myself, that tendency must have been so completely neutralized by the redundant moral energy inherent in his nature, that the characteristic effect which I should have ascribed to them is absolutely unverifiable, and, for anything we have the right to assert, non-existent. There is at least but one instance in which I should have traced any shade of what

I may call the natural view of death as presented in the
light of this creed, and that is the sentence in which Mr.
Harrison somewhat superfluously disclaims—and, moreover, with an accent of *hauteur*, as though he resented
the necessity of admitting that death is a disagreeable
certainty—his own or his creed's responsibility for the
fact of death. "We make no mystical or fanciful divinity
of death," he says: "we do not deny its terrors or its
evils. We are not responsible for it, and should welcome
any reasonable prospect of eliminating or postponing this
fatality that waits upon all organic nature." After reading that admission, I was puzzled when I came to the
assertion that "we who know that a higher form of
activity is only to be reached by a subjective life in
society, will continue to regard a perpetuity of sensation
as the true hell," a sentence in which Mr. Harrison would
commonly be understood to mean that he and all his
friends, if they had a vote in the matter, would give a
unanimous suffrage against this "perpetuity of sensation,"
and, so far from trying to eliminate and postpone death,
would be inclined to cling to and even hasten it. For, in
this place at least, it is not the perpetuation of deteriora-
ted energies of which Mr. Harrison speaks, but the
perpetuation of life pure and simple. Indeed, nothing
puzzles me more in this paper than the diametrical contradictions, both of feeling and thought, which appear to
me to be embodied in it. Its main criticism on the common view of immortality seems to be that the desire for it
is a grossly selfish desire. Nay, nicknaming the conception

of a future of eternal praise, "the eternity of the tabor,"
he calls it a conception "so gross, so sensual, so indolent,
so selfish," as to be worthy of nothing but scorn. I think
he can never have taken the trouble to realize with any
care what he is talking of. Whatever the conception
embodied in what Mr. Harrison calls "ceaseless psalmody,"
may be—and certainly it is not my idea of immortal life
—it is the very opposite of selfish. No conception of life
can be selfish of which the very essence is adoration, that
is, wonder, veneration, gratitude to another. And gross
as the conception necessarily suggested by psalm-singing is
to those who interpret it, as we generally do, by the sten-
torian shoutings of congregations who are often thinking
a great deal more of their own performances than of the
object of their praise, it is the commonest candour to
admit that this conception of immortality owes its origin
entirely to men who were thinking of a life absorbed in
the interior contemplation of a God full of all perfections
—a contemplation breaking out into thanksgiving only
in the intensity of their love and adoration. Whatever
else this conception of immortality may be, the very last
phrase which can be justly applied to it is "gross" or
"selfish." I fear that the positivists have left the
Christian objects of their criticism so far behind that they
have ceased not merely to realize what Christians mean,
but have sincerely and completely forgotten that Christians ever had a meaning at all. That positivists should
regard any belief in the "beatific vision" as a wild piece of
fanaticism, I can understand, but that, entering into the

meaning of that fanaticism, they should describe the
desire for it as a gross piece of selfishness, I cannot understand ; and I think it more reasonable, therefore, to assume
that they have simply lost the key to the language of
adoration.   Moreover, when I come to note Mr. Harrison's
own conception of the future life, it appears to me that it
differs only from the Christian's conception by its infinite
deficiencies, and in no respect by superior moral qualities
of any kind.   That conception, is in a word, posthumous
energy.   He holds that if we could get rid of the vulgar
notion of a survival of personal sensations and of growing
mental and moral faculties after death, we should consecrate the notion of posthumous activity, and anticipate
with delight our " coming incorporation with the glorious
future of our race," as we cannot possibly consecrate
those great hopes now.

But, in the first place, what is this "glorious future of
our race " which I am invited to contemplate ?   It is the
life in a better organized society of a vast number of these
merely temporary creatures whose personal sensations, if
they ever could be " perpetuated," Mr. Harrison regards
as giving us the best conception of a "true hell."   Now
if an improved and better organized future of ephemerals
be so glorious to anticipate, what elements of glory are
there in it which would not belong to the immortality
looked forward to by the Christian—a far more improved
future of endlessly growing natures ?   Is it the mere fact
that I shall myself belong to the one future which renders
it unworthy, while the absence of any " perpetuity" of my

5

personal "sensations" from the other renders it unselfish ?
I always supposed selfishness to consist, *not* in the desire
for any noble kind of life in which I might share, but in
the preference for my own happiness at the *expense* of
some one else's. If it is selfish to desire the perpetuation
of a growing life, which not only does not, as far as I know,
interfere with the volume of moral growth in others, but
certainly contributes to it, then it must be the true unselfishness to commit suicide at once, supposing suicide to
be the *finis* to personal "sensation." But then universal
suicide would be inconsistent with the glorious future of
our race, so I suppose it must at least be postponed till our
own sensations have been so far "perpetuated " as to leave
heirs behind them. If Condorcet is to be held up to our
admiration for anticipating on the edge of the grave his
"coming incorporation with the glorious future of his
race," *i. e.*, with ourselves and our posterity, may we not
infer that there is something in ourselves, *i. e.*, in human
society as it now exists, which is worthy of his vision—
something in which we need not think it "selfish " to
participate, even though our personal "sensations" do
form a part of it ? Where, then, does the selfishness of
desiring to share in a glorious future even through personal "sensations" begin? The only reasonable or
even intelligible answer, as far as I can see, is this: as
soon as that personal "sensation "for ourselves excludes a
larger and wider growth for others, but no sooner. But
then no Christian ever supposed for a moment that his
personal immortality could or would interfere with any

other being's growth. And, if so, where is the selfishness ? What a Christian desires is a higher, truer, deeper union with God for all, himself included. If his own life drop out of that future, he supposes that there will be so much less that really does glorify the true righteousness, and no compensating equivalent. If it be Mr. Harrison's mission to disclose to us that any perpetuity of sensation on our own parts will positively exclude something much higher which *would* exist if we consented to disappear, he may, I think, prove his case. But in the absence of any attempt to do so, his conception that it is noble and unselfish to be more than content—grateful—for ceasing to live any but a posthumous life seems to me simply irrational.

But, further, the equivalent which Mr. Harrison offers me for becoming, as I had hoped to become in another world, an altogether better member of a better society, does not seem to me more than a very doubtful good. My posthumous activity will be of all kinds, some of which I am glad to anticipate, most of which I am very sorry to anticipate, and much of which I anticipate with absolute indifference. Even our best actions have bad effects, as well as good. Macaulay and most other historians held that the Puritan earnestness expended a good deal of posthumous activity in producing the license of the world of the Restoration. Our activity, indeed, is strictly posthumous in kind, even before our death from the very moment in which it leaves our living mind and has begun to work beyond ourselves. What I did as a child is, in this sense, as much producing posthumous effects, *i. e.*, effects over which I can no longer exert any control, now, as what I do before death will be producing posthumous effects after my death. Now, a considerable proportion of these posthumous activities of ours, even when we can justify the original activity as all that it ought to have been, are unfortunate. Mr. Harrison's papers, for instance, have already exerted a very vivid and very repulsive effect on my mind—an activity which I am sure he will not look upon with gratification, and I do not doubt that what I am now writing will produce the same effect on him, and in that effect I shall take no delight at all. A certain proportion, therefore, of my posthumous activity is activity for evil, even when the activity itself is on the whole good. But when we come to throw in the posthumous activity for evil exerted by our evil actions and the occasional posthumous activity for good which evil also fortunately exerts, but for the good results of which we can take no credit to ourselves, the whole constitutes a *mélange* to which, as far as I am concerned, I look with exceedingly mixed feelings, the chief element being humiliation, though there are faint lights mingled with it here and there. But as for any rapture of satisfaction in contemplating my "coming incorporation with the glorious future of our race," I must wholly and entirely disclaim it. What I see in that incorporation of mine with the future of our race—glorious or the reverse, and I do not quite see why the positivist thinks it so glorious, since he probably holds that an absolute term must be put to

it, if by no other cause, by the gradual cooling of the sun
—is a very patchwork sort of affair indeed, a mere
miscellany of bad, good, and indifferent, without organization and without unity. What I shall be, for instance,
when incorporated, in Mr. Harrison's phrase, with the
future of our race, I have very little satisfaction in contemplating except so far, perhaps, as my " posthumous
activity " may retard the acceptance of Mr. Harrison's
glorious anticipations for the human race. One great
reason for my personal wish for a perpetuity of volition
and personal energy is, that I may have a better opportunity, as far as may lie in me, to undo the mischief I shall
have done before death comes to my aid. The vision of
" posthumous activity " ought indeed, I fancy, to give even
the best of us very little satisfaction. It may not be, and
perhaps is not, so mischievous as the vision of " posthumous fame," but yet it is not the kind of vision which, to
my mind, can properly occupy very much of our attention
in this life. Surely, the right thing for us to do is to concentrate attention on the life of the living moment—to
make that the best we can—and then to leave its posthumous effects, after the life of the present has gone out of
it, to that power which, far more than anything in it, trans-
mutes at times even our evil into good, though sometimes,
too, to superficial appearance at all events, even our good
into evil. The desire for an immortal life—that is, for a
perpetuation of the personal affections and of the will—
seems to me a far nobler thing than any sort of anticipation as to our posthumous activity ; for high affections

and a right will are good in *themselves,* and constitute, indeed, the only elements in Mr. Harrison's " glorious future of our race " to which I can attach much value— while posthumous activity may be either good or evil, and depends on conditions over which he who first puts the activity in motion often has no adequate control.

And this reminds me of a phrase in Mr. Harrison's paper, which I have studied over and over again without making out his meaning. I mean his statement that on his own hypothesis "there is ample scope for the spiritual life, for moral responsibility, for the world beyond the grave, *its hopes and its duties,* which remain to us perfectly real without the unintelligible hypothesis." Now, I suppose, by " the hopes " of the " world beyond the grave," Mr. Harrison means the hopes we form *for* the " future of our race," and that I understand. But what does he mean by its " duties ? " Not, surely, our duties beyond the grave, but the duties of those who survive us ; for he expressly tells us that our mental and moral powers do not increase and grow, develop or vary within themselves—do not, in fact, survive at all except in their effects —and hence duties for *us* in the world beyond the grave are, I suppose, in his creed impossible. But if he only means that there will be duties for those who survive us after we are gone, I cannot see how that is in any respect a theme on which it is either profitable or consolatory for us to dwell by anticipation. One remark more : When Mr. Harrison says that it is quite as easy to learn to long for the moment when you shall become " the immaterial principle of a comet," or that you " really were the

ether, and were about to take your place in space," as to
long for personal immortality—he is merely talking at
random on a subject on which it is hardly seemly to talk
at random.　He knows that what we mean by the soul is
that which lies at the bottom of the sense of personal
identity—the thread of the continuity running through
all our checkered life ; and how it can be equally unmeaning to believe that this hitherto unbroken continuity
will continue unbroken, and to believe that it is to be
transformed into something else of a totally different
kind, I am not only unable to understand, but even to
understand how he could seriously so conceive us.　My
notion of myself never had the least connection with the
principle of any part of any comet, but it has the closest
possible connection with thoughts, affections, and volitions, which, as far as I know, are not likely to perish
with my body.　I am sorry that Mr. Harrison should
have disfigured his paper by sarcasms so inapplicable and
apparently so bitter as these.

PROF. HUXLEY.

M R. HARRISON'S striking discourse on "The Soul
and Future Life" has a certain resemblance to the
famous essay on the snakes of Iceland.　For its purport is to
show that there is no soul, nor any future life, in the ordinary
sense of the terms.　With death, the personal activity of which

the soul is the popular hypostasis is put into commission among posterity, and the future life is an immortality by deputy.

Neither in these views nor in the arguments by which they are supported is there much novelty. But that which appears both novel and interesting to me is the author's evidently sincere and heart-felt conviction that his powerful advocacy of soulless spirituality and mortal immortality is consistent with the intellectual scorn and moral reprobation which he freely pours forth upon the "irrational and debasing physicism" of materialism and materialists, and with the wrath with which he visits what he is pleased to call the intrusion of physical science, especially of biology, into the domain of social phenomena.

Listen to the storm:

"We certainly do reject, as earnestly as any school can, that which is most fairly called materialism, and we will second every word of those who cry out that civilization is in danger if the workings of the human spirit are to become questions of physiology, and if death is the end of a man, as it is the end of a sparrow. We not only assent to such protests, but we see very pressing need for making them. It is a corrupting doctrine to open a brain, and to tell us that devotion is a definite molecular change in this and that convolution of gray pulp, and that, if man is the first of living animals, he passes away after a short space like the beasts that perish. And all doctrines, more or less, do tend to this, which offer physical theories as explaining moral phenomena, which deny man a spiritual in addition to a moral nature, which limit his moral life to the span of his bodily organism, and which have no place for 'religion' in the proper sense of the word."

Now, Mr. Harrison can hardly think it worth while to attack imaginary opponents, so that I am led to believe that there must be somebody who holds the " corrupting doctrine," " that devotion is a definite molecular change in this and that convolution of gray pulp." Nevertheless, my conviction is shaken by this passage : " No rational thinker now pretends that imagination *is* simply the vibration of a particular fibre." If no rational thinker pretends this of imagination, why should any pretend it of devotion ? And yet I cannot bring myself to think that all Mr. Harrison's passionate rhetoric is hurled at irrational thinkers: surely he might leave such to the soft influences of time and due medical treatment of their " gray pulp " in Colney Hatch or elsewhere.

On the other hand, Mr. Harrison cannot possibly be attacking those who hold that the feeling of devotion is the concomitant, or even the consequent, of a molecular change in the brain ; for he tells us, in language the explicitness of which leaves nothing to be desired, that

" To positive methods every fact of thinking reveals itself as having functional relation with molecular change. Every factor of will or feeling is in similar relation with kindred molecular facts. '

On mature consideration, I feel shut up to one or two alternative hypotheses. Either the " corrupting doctrine " to which Mr. Harrison refers is held by no rational thinker—in which case, surely, neither he nor I need trouble ourselves about it—or the phrase " Devotion *is* a definite molecular change in this and that convolution of

gray pulp," means that devotion has a functional relation
with such molecular change : in which case it is Mr. Harrison's own view, and therefore, let us hope, cannot be a
" corrupting doctrine."

I am not helped out of the difficulty I have thus
candidly stated, when I try to get at the meaning of
another hard saying of Mr. Harrison's, which follows
after the "corrupting doctrine" paragraph : "And all
doctrines, more or less, do tend to this [corrupting doc-
trine], which offer physical theories as explaining moral
phenomena."

Nevertheless, Mr. Harrison says, with great force and
tolerable accuracy :

"Man is one, however compound. Fire his conscience and he
blushes. Check his circulation and he thinks wildly, or thinks not
at all. Impair his secretions, and moral sense is dulled, discoloured,
or depraved ; his aspirations flag ; his hope, love, faith, reel. Impair
them still more, and he becomes a brute. A cup of drink degrades
his moral nature below that of a swine. Again, a violent emotion
of pity or horror makes him vomit. A lancet will restore him from
delirium to clear thought. Excess of thought will waste his sinews ;
excess of muscular exercise will deaden thought. An emotion will
double the strength of his muscles ; and at last the prick of a needle
or a grain of mineral will in an instant lay to rest forever his body
and its unity, and all the spontaneous activities of intelligence,
feeling, and action, with which that compound organism was
charged.

" These are the obvious and ancient observations about the human
organism. But modern philosophy and science have carried these
hints into complete explanations. By a vast accumulation of proof
positive, thought at last has established a distinct correspondence

between every process of thought or of feeling, and some corporeal phenomenon."

I cry with Shylock:

"'Tis very true, O wise and upright judge."

But, if the establishment of the correspondence between physical phenomena on the one side, and moral and intellectual phenomena on the other, is properly to be called an *explanation* (let alone a *complete explanation*), of the human organism, surely Mr. Harrison's teachings come dangerously near that tender of physical theories in explanation of moral phenomena which he warns us leads straight to corruption.

But perhaps I have misinterpreted Mr. Harrison; for a few lines further on we are told, with due italic emphasis, that no man can explain volition by purely anatomical study." I should have thought that Mr. Harrison might have gone much further than this. No man ever explained any physiological fact by purely anatomical study. Digestion cannot be so explained, nor respiration, nor reflex action. It would have been as relevant to affirm that volition could not be explained by measuring an arc of the meridian.

I am obliged to note the fact that Mr. Harrison's biological studies have not proceeded so far as to enable him to discriminate between the province of anatomy and that of physiology, because it furnishes the key to an otherwise mysterious utterance which occurs thus:

"A man whose whole thoughts are absorbed in cutting up dead

monkeys and live frogs, has no more business to dogmatize about religion than a mere chemist to improvise a zoölogy."

Quis negavit ? But if, as, on Mr. Harrison's own show-ing, is the case, the progress of science (not anatomical, but physiological) has "established a distinct correspond-ence between every process of thought or of feeling, and some corporeal phenomenon," and if it is true that "im-paired secretions" deprave the moral sense, and make "hope, love, and faith reel," surely the religious feelings are brought within the range of physiological inquiry. If impaired secretions deprave the moral sense, it becomes an interesting and important problem to ascertain what diseased viscus may have been responsible for the *priest in absolution;* and what condition of the gray pulp may have conferred on it such a pathological steadiness of faith as to create the hope of personal immortality, which Mr. Harrison stigmatizes as so selfishly immoral.

I should not like to undertake the responsibility of advising anybody to dogmatize about anything; but surely if, as Mr. Harrison so strongly urges, "the whole range of man's powers, from the finest spiritual sensibility down to a mere automatic contraction, falls into one co-herent scheme, being all the multiform functions of a living organism in presence of its encircling conditions," then the man who endeavours to ascertain the exact nature of these functions, and to determine the influence of conditions upon them, is more likely to be in a position to tell us something worth hearing about them, than one who is turned from such study by cheap pulpit thunder touching the presumption of "biological reasoning about spiritual things."

Mr. Harrison, as we have seen, is not quite so clear as is desirable respecting the limits of the provinces of anatomy and physiology. Perhaps he will permit me to inform him that physiology is the science which treats of the functions of the living organism, ascertains their coördinations and their correlations in the general chain of causes and effects, and traces out their dependence upon the physical state of the organs by which these functions are exercised. The explanation of a physiological function is the demonstration of the connection of that function with the molecular state of the organ which exerts the function. Thus the function of motion is explained when the movements of the living body are found to have certain molecular changes for their invariable antecedents; the function of sensation is explained when the molecular changes, which are the invariable antecedents of sensations, are discovered.

The fact that it is impossible to comprehend how it is that a physical state gives rise to a mental state, no more lessens the value of the explanation in the latter case, than the fact that it is utterly impossible to comprehend how motion is communicated from one body to another weakens the force of the explanation of the motion of one billiard-ball by showing that another has hit it.

"The finest spiritual sensibility," says Mr. Harrison (and I think that there is a fair presumption that he is right), is a function of a living organism—is in relation with molecular facts. In that case the physiologist may reply : "It is my business to find out what these molecular facts are, and whether the relation between them and the said spiritual sensibility is one of antecedence in the molecular fact, and sequence in the spiritual fact, or *vice versa*. If the latter result comes out of my inquiries, I shall have made a contribution toward a moral theory of physical phenomena ; if the former, I shall have done somewhat toward building up a physical theory of moral phenomena. But in any case I am not outstepping the limits of my proper province ; my business is to get at the truth respecting such questions at all risks ; and if you tell me that one of these two results is a corrupting doctrine, I can only say that I perceive the intended reproach conveyed by the observation, but that I fail to recognize its relevance. If the doctrine is true, its social septic or antiseptic properties are not my affair. My business as a biologist is with physiology, not with morals."

This plea of justification strikes me as complete; whence, then, the following outbreak of angry eloquence ?—

" The arrogant attempt to dispose of the deepest moral truths of human nature, on a bare physical or physiological basis, is almost enough to justify the insurrection of some impatient theologians against science itself."

" That strain again : it has a dying fall ;" nowise similar to the sweet south upon a bank of violets, however, but like the death-wail of innumerable " impatient theologians," as from the high " drum ecclesiastic " they view the waters of science flooding the Church on all hands.

The beadles have long been washed away ; escape by pulpit stairs is even becoming doubtful, without kirtling
those outward investments which distinguish the priest
from the man so high, that no one will see that there is
anything but the man left. But Mr. Harrison is not an
impatient theologian—indeed, no theologian at all, unless,
as he speaks of "soul" when he means certain bodily
functions, and of "future life" when he means personal
annihilation, he may make his master's *grand être suprême*
the subject of a theology ; and one stumbles upon this
well-worn fragment of too-familiar declamation among his
vigorous periods with the unpleasant surprise of one who
finds a fly in a precious ointment.

There are people from whom one does not expect well-
founded statement and thoughtful, however keen, argu-
mentation, embodied in precise language ; from Mr.
Harrison one does. But I think he will be at a loss to
answer the question, if I pray him to tell me of any
representative of physical science who, either arrogantly
or otherwise, has ever attempted to dispose of moral truths
on a physical or physiological basis. If I am to take the
sense of the words literally, I shall not dispute the arrogance of the attempt to dispose of a moral truth on a bare,
or even on a covered, physical or physiological basis ; for,
whether the truth is deep or shallow, I cannot conceive
how the feat is to be performed. Columbus's difficulty
with the egg is as nothing to it. But I suppose what is
meant is, that some arrogant people have tried to upset
morality by the help of physics and physiology. I am

sorry if such people exist, because I shall have to be much ruder to them than Mr. Harrison is. I should not call them arrogant, any more than I should apply that epithet to a person who attempted to upset Euclid by the help of the Rig-Veda. Accuracy might be satisfied, if not propriety, by calling such a person a fool; but it appears to me that it would be the height of injustice to term him arrogant.

Whatever else they may be, the laws of morality, under their scientific aspect, are generalizations based upon the observed phenomena of society; and, whatever may be the nature of moral approbation and disapprobation, these feelings are, as matter of experience, associated with certain acts.

The consequences of men's actions will remain the same, however far our analysis of the causes which lead to them may be pushed; theft and murder would be none the less objectionable if it were possible to prove that they were the result of the activity of special theft and murder cells in that "gray pulp" of which Mr. Harrison speaks so scornfully. Does any sane man imagine that any quantity of physiological analysis will lead people to think breaking their legs or putting their hands into the fire desirable? And when men really believe that breaches of the moral law involve their penalties as surely as do breaches of the physical law, is it to be supposed that even the very firmest disposal of their moral truths upon "a bare physical or physiological basis" will tempt them to incur those penalties?

I would gladly learn from Mr. Harrison where, in the

course of his studies, he has found anything inconsistent with what I have just said in the writings of physicists or biologists. I would entreat him to tell us who are the true materialists, "the scientific specialists" who "neglect all philosophical and religious synthesis," and who "submit religion to the test of the scalpel or the electric battery;" where the materialism which is "marked by the ignoring of religion, the passing by on the other side and shutting the eyes to the spiritual history of mankind," is to be found.

I will not believe that these phrases are meant to apply to any scientific men of whom I have cognizance, or to any recognized system of scientific thought—they would be too absurdly inappropriate—and I cannot believe that Mr. Harrison indulges in empty rhetoric. But I am disposed to think that they would not have been used at all, except for that deep-seated sympathy with the "impatient theologian" which characterizes the positivist school, and crops out, characteristically enough, in more than one part of Mr. Harrison's essay.

Mr. Harrison tells us that "positivism is prepared to meet the theologians." I agree with him, though not exactly in his sense of the words—indeed, I have formerly expressed the opinion that the meeting took place long ago, and that the faithful lovers, impelled by the instinct of a true affinity of nature, have met to part no more. Ecclesiastical to the core from the beginning, positivism is now exemplifying the law that the outward garment adjusts itself, sooner or later, to the inward man. From its

6

founder onward, striken with metaphysical incompetence,
and equally incapable of appreciating the true spirit of
scientific method, it is now essaying to cover the naked-
ness of its philosophical materialism with the rags of a
spiritualistic phraseology out of which the original sense
has wholly departed. I understand and I respect the
meaning of the word "soul," as used by Pagan and Christian philosophers for what they believe to be the imperishable seat of human personality, bearing throughout
eternity its burden of woe, or its capacity for adoration.
and love. I confess that my dull moral sense does not
enable me to see anything base or selfish in the desire for
a future life among the spirits of the just made perfect ;
or even among a few such poor fallible souls as one has
known here below.

And if I am not satisfied with the evidence that is
offered me that such a soul and such a future life exists,
I am content to take what is to be had and to make the
best of the brief span of existence that is within my reach,
without reviling those whose faith is more robust and
whose hopes are richer and fuller. But in the interest of
scientific clearness, I object to say that I have a soul, when
I mean, all the while, that my organism has certain mental
functions which, like the rest, are dependent upon its
molecular composition, and come to an end when I die ;
and I object still more to affirm that I look to a future
life, when all that I mean is, that the influence of my say-
ings and doings will be more or less felt by a number of

people after the physical components of that organism are scattered to the four winds.

Throw a stone into the sea, and there is a sense in which it is true that the wavelets which spread around it have an effect through all space and all time. Shall we say that the stone has a future life?

It is not worth while to have broken away, not without pain and grief, from beliefs which, true or false, embody great and fruitful conceptions, to fall back into the arms of a half-breed, between science and theology, endowed, like most half-breeds, with the faults of both parents and the virtues of neither. And it is unwise by such a lapse to expose one's self to the temptation of holding with the hare and hunting with the hounds—of using the weapons of one progenitor to damage the other. I cannot but think that the members of the positivist school in this country stand in some danger of falling into that fatal error; and I put it to them to consider whether it is either consistent or becoming for those who hold that the "finest spiritual sensibility" is a mere bodily function, to join in the view-halloo, when the hunt is up against biological science— to use their voices in swelling the senseless cry that "civilization is in danger if the workings of the human spirit are to become questions of physiology."

LORD BLACHFORD.

M R. HARRISON is of opinion that the difference between Christians and himself on this question of
the soul and the future life, " turns altogether on habits of
thought." What appears to the positivist flimsy will, he
says, seem to the Christian sublime, and *vice versa*," simply
because our minds have been trained in different logical
methods,"and this apparently because positivism"pretends
to no other basis than positive knowledge and scientific
logic." But if this is so, it is not, I think, quite consistent
to conclude, as he does, that " it is idle to dispute about our
respective logical methods, or to put this or that habit of
mind in a combat with that." As to the combatants this
may be true. But it surely is not idle, but very much to the
purpose, for the information of those judges to whom the
very act of publication appeals, to discuss habits and me;
thods on which, it is declared, the difference altogether
turns.

I note, therefore, *in limine* what, as I go on, I shall
have occasion to illustrate, one or two differences between
the methods of Mr. Harrison and those in which I have
been trained.

I have been taught to consider that certain words or
ideas represent what are called by logicians substances, by
Mr. Harrison, I think, entities, and by others, as the case
may be, persons, beings, objects, or articles. Such are air,
earth, man, horses, chairs, and tables. Their peculiarity

is that they have each of them a separate, independent, substantive existence. They *are*.

There are other words or ideas which do not represent existing things, but qualities, relations, consequences, processes, or occurrences, like victory, virtue, life, order, or destruction, which do but belong to substances, or result from them without any distinct existence of their own. A thing signified by a word of the former class cannot possibly be identical or even homogeneous with a thing signified by a word of the second class. A fiddle is not only a different thing from a tune, but it' belongs to another and totally distinct order of ideas. To this distinction the English mind at some period of its history must have been imperfectly alive. If a Greek confounded κτίσις with κτίσμα, an act with a thing, it was the fault of the individual. But the English language, instead of precluding such a confusion, almost, one would say, labours to propagate it. Such words as "building," "announcement," "preparation," or "power," are equally available to signify either the act of construction or an edifice—either the act of proclaiming or a placard—either the act of preparing or a surgical specimen—either the ability to do something or the being in which that ability resides. Such imperfections of language infuse themselves into thought. And I venture to think that the slight superciliousness with which Mr. Harrison treats the doctrines, which such persons as myself entertain respecting the soul is in some degree due to the fact that positive " habits of thought " and " logical methods," do not recognize so completely as ours the distinction which I have described as that between a fiddle and a tune.

Again, my own habit of mind is to distinguish more pointedly than Mr. Harrison does between a unit and a complex whole. When I speak of an act of individual will, I seem to myself to speak of an indivisible act proceeding from a single being. The unity is not merely in my mode of representation, but in the thing signified. If I speak of an act of the national will—say a determination to declare war—I speak of the concurrence of a number of individual wills, each acting for itself, and under an infinite variety of influences, but so related to each other and so acting in concert that it is convenient to represent them under the aggregate term " nation." I use a term which signifies unity of being, but I really mean nothing more than coöperation, or correlated action and feeling. So, when I speak of the happiness of humanity, I mean nothing whatever but a number of particular happinesses of individual persons. Humanity is not a unit, but a word which enables me to bring a number of units under view at once. In the case of material objects, I apprehend, unity is simply relative and artificial—a grain of corn is a unit relatively to a bushel, and an aggregate relatively to an atom. But I, believing myself to be a spiritual being, call myself actually and without metaphor—one.

Mr. Harrison, who acknowledges the existence of no being but matter, appears either to deny the existence of any real unity whatever, or to ascribe the real unity to an aggregate of things or beings who resemble each other,

like the members of the human race, or coöperate toward
a common result, like the parts of a picture, a melody, or
the human frame, and which may thus be conveniently
viewed in combination, and represented by a single word
or phrase.

I think that the little which I have to say will be the
clearer for these preliminary protests.

The questions in hand relate first to the claim of the
soul of man to be treated as an existing thing not bound
by the laws of matter: secondly to the immortality of
that existing thing.

The claim of the soul to be considered as an existing
and immaterial being presents itself to my mind as
follows:

My positive experience informs me of one thing percipient—myself; and of a multitude of things perceptible—perceptible, that is, not by way of consciousness,
as I am to myself, but by way of impression on other
things—capable of making themselves felt through the
channels and organs of sensation. These things thus perceptible constitute the material world.

I take no account of percipients other than myself, for
I can only conjecture about them what I know about
myself. I take no account of things neither percipient
nor perceptible, for it is impossible to do so. I know of
nothing outside me of which I can say it is at once percipient and perceptible. But I enquire whether I am
myself so—whether the existing being to which my sense
of identity refers, in which my sensations reside, and

which for these two reasons I call "myself," is capable also of being perceived by beings outside myself, as the material world is perceived by me.

I first observe that things perceptible comprise not only objects, but instruments and media of perception—an immense variety of contrivances, natural or artificial, for transmitting information to the sensitive being. Such are telescopes, microscopes, ear-trumpets, the atmosphere, and various other media which, if not at present the objects of direct sensation, may conceivably become so—and such, above all, are various parts of the human body —the lenses which collect the vibrations which are the conditions of light; the tympanum which collects the vibrations which are the conditions of sound; the muscles which adjust these and other instruments of sensation to the precise performance of their work; the nerves which convey to and fro molecular movements of the most incomprehensible significance and efficacy. Of all these it is, I understand, more and more evident, as science advances, that they are perceptible, but do not perceive. Ear, hand, eye, and nerves, are alike machinery—mere machinery for transmitting the movement of atoms to certain nervous centres—ascertained localities which (it is proper to observe in passing), though small relatively to ourselves and our powers of investigation, may—since size is entirely relative—be *absolutely* large enough to contain little worlds in themselves.

Here the investigation of things perceptible is stopped, abruptly and completely. Our inquiries into the size,

composition and movement of particles, have been pushed, for the present at any rate, as far as they will go.
But at this point we come across a field of phenomena to
which the attributes of atoms, size, movement, and physical composition, are wholly inapplicable—the phenomena
of sensation or animal life.

Science informs me that the movements of these perceptible atoms within my body bear a correspondence,
strange, subtle, and precise, to the sensations of which I,
as a percipient, am conscious ; a correspondence (it is again
proper to observe in passing) which extends not only to
perceptions, as in sight or hearing, but to reflection and
volition, as in sleep and drunkenness. The relation is
not one of similarity. The vibrations of a white, black,
or gray pulp are not in any sensible way similar to the
perception of colour or sound, or the imagination of a noble
act. There is no visible—may I not say no conceivable ?
—reason why one should depend on the other. Motion
and sensation interact, but they do not overlap. There
is no homogeneity between them. They stand apart.
Physical science conducts us to the brink of the chasm
which separates them, and by so doing only shews us its
depth.

I return then to the question, "What am I?" My
own habits of mind and logical methods certainly require
me to believe that I am something—something percipient
—but am I perceptible ? I find no reason for supposing it.
I believe myself to be surrounded by things percipient.
Are they perceptible ? Not to my knowledge. Their

existence is to me a matter of inference from their perceptible appendages. Them—their very selves—I certainly cannot perceive. As far as I can understand things perceptible, I detect in them no quality—no capacity for any quality like that of percipiency, which, with its homogeneous faculties, intellect, affections, and so on, is the basis of my own nature. Physical science, while it develops the relation, seems absolutely to emphasize and illuminate the ineradicable difference between the motions of a material and the sensations of a living being. Of the attributes of a percipient we have, each for himself, profound and immediate experience. Of the attributes of the perceptible we have, I suppose, distinct scientific conceptions. Our notions of the one and our notions of the other appear to attach to a different order of being.

It appears therefore to me that there is no reason to believe, and much reason for not believing, that the percipient is perceptible under our present conditions of existence, or indeed under any conditions that our present faculties enable us to imagine.

And this is my case, which of course covers the whole animal creation. Perception must be an attribute of something; and there is reason for believing that this something is imperceptible. This is what I mean when I say that I have, or more properly that I am, a soul or a spirit, or rather it is the point on which I join issue with those who say that I am not.

I am not, as Mr. Harrison seems to suppose, running

about in search of a " cause." I am inquiring into the
nature of a being, and that being myself. I am sure I
am something. I am certainly not the mere tangible
structure of atoms which I affect, and by which I am affected after a wonderful fashion. In reflecting on the
nature of my own operations I find nothing to suggest
that my own being is subject to the same class of physical laws as the objects from which my sensations are derived, and I conclude that I am not subject to those laws.
The most substantial objection to this conclusion is conveyed, I conceive, in a sentence of Mr. Harrison's: "To
talk to us of mind, feeling and will, continuing their
functions in the absence of physical organs and visible
organisms, is to use language which, to us at least, is pure
nonsense."

It is probably to those who talk thus that Mr. Harrison
refers when he says that argument is useless. And in
point of fact I have no answer but to call his notions
anthropomorphic, and to charge him with want of a certain kind of imagination. By imagination we commonly
mean the creative faculty which enables a man to give a
palpable shape to what he believes or thinks possible ;
and this, I do not doubt, Mr. Harrison possesses in a high
degree. But there is another kind of imagination which
enables a man to embrace the idea of a possibility to
which no such palpable shape can be given, or rather of
a world of possibilities beyond the range of his experience or the grasp of his faculties; as Mr. John Mill em-
braced the idea of a possible world in which the connec-

tion of cause and effect should not exist. The want of this necessary though dangerous faculty makes a man the victim of vivid impressions, and disables him from believing what his impressions do not enable him to realize. Questions respecting metaphysical possibility turn much on the presence, or absence, or exaggeration, of this kind of imagination. And when one man has said, " I can perceive it possible," and another has said, "I cannot," it is certainly difficult to get any further.

To me it is not in the slightest degree difficult to conceive the possible existence of a being capable of love and knowledge without the physical organs through which human beings derive their knowledge, nor in supposing myself to be such a being. Indeed, I seem actually to exercise such a capacity (however I got it) when I shut my eyes and try to think out a moral or mathematical puzzle. If it is true that a particular corner of my brain is concerned in the matter, I accept the fact not as a self-evident truth (which would seem to be Mr. Harrison's position), but as a curious discovery of the anatomists. But having said this I have said everything, and, as Mr. Harrison must suppose that I deceive myself, so I suppose that in his case the imagination which founds itself on experience is so active and vivid as to cloud or dwarf the imagination which proceeds beyond or beside experience.

Mr. Harrison's own theory I do not quite understand. He derides the idea, though he does not absolutely deny the possibility, of an immaterial entity which feels. And he appears to be sensible of the difficulty of supposing that atoms of matter which assume the form of a gray pulp can feel. He holds accordingly, as I understand, that feeling, and all that follows from it, are the results of an " organism."

If he had used the word " organization," I should have concluded unhesitatingly that he was the victim of the Anglican confusion which I have above noticed, and that in his own mind, he escaped the alternative difficulties of the case by the common expedient of shifting as occasion required from one sense of that word to the other. If pressed by the difficulty of imagining sensation not resident in any specific sensitive thing, the word organization would supply to his mind the idea of a thing, a sensitive aggregate of organized atoms. If, on the contrary, pressed by the difficulty of supposing that these atoms, one or all, thought, the word would shift its meaning and present the aspect not of an aggregate bulk, but of orderly arrangement—not of a thing, or a collection of things, but of a state of things. •

But the word " organism " is generally taken to indicate a thing organized. And the choice of that word would seem to indicate that he ascribed the spiritual acts (so to call them) which constitute life to the aggregate bulk of the atoms organized, or the appropriate part of them. But this he elsewhere seems to disclaim. " The philosophy which treats man as man simply affirms that *man* loves, thinks, acts, not that ganglia, or the sinews, or any organ of man loves, and thinks, and acts." Yes, but we recur to the question, "What is man?" If the ganglia do not think, what is it that does? Mr. Harrison, as I understand, answers that it is a *consensus* of faculties, an harmonious system of parts, and he denounces an attempt to introduce into this collocation of parts or faculties an underlying entity or being which shall possess those faculties or employ those parts. It is then not after all to a being or aggregate of beings, but to a relation or condition of beings, that will and thought and love belong. If this is Mr. Harrison's meaning, I certainly agree with him that it is indeed impossible to compose a difference between two disputants of whom one holds, and the other denies, that a condition can think. If my opponent does not admit this to be an absurdity, I do not pretend to drive him any further.

With regard to immortality, I have nothing material to add to what has been said by those who have preceded me. I agree with Prof. Huxley that the natural world supplies nothing which can be called evidence of a future life. Believing in God, I see in the constitution of the world which he has made, and in the yearnings and aspirations of that spiritual nature which he has given to man, much that commends to my belief the revelation of a future life which I believe him to have made. But it is in virtue of his clear promise, not in virtue of these doubtful intimations, that I rely on the prospect of a future life. Believing that he is the author of that moral insight which in its ruder forms controls the multitude, and in its higher inspires the saint, I revere those great men who were able to forecast this great announcement, but I cannot and do not care to reduce that forecast to any logical process, or base it on any conclusive reasoning. Rather I admire their power of divination the more on account of the narrowness of their logical data. For myself, I believe because I am told.

But whether the doctrine of immortality be true or false, I protest, with Mr. Hutton, against the attempt to substitute for what, at any rate, is a substantial idea, something which can hardly be called even a shadow or echo of it.

The Christian conception of the world is this : It is a world of moral as of physical waste. Much seed is sown which will not ripen, but some is sown that will. This planet is a seat, among other things, of present goodness and happiness. And this our goodness and happiness, like our crime and misery, propagate or fail to propagate themselves during our lives and after our deaths. But, apart from these earthly consequences, which are much to us and all to the positivist, the little fragment of the universe on which we appear and disappear is, we believe, a nursery for something greater. The capacities for love and knowledge, which in some of us attain a certain development here, we must all feel to be capable, with greater opportunities, of an infinitely greater development; and Christians believe that such a development is in fact reserved for those who, in this short time of apprenticeship, take the proper steps for approaching it.

This conception of a glorious and increasing company,

into which the best of men are continually to be gathered
to be associated with each other (to say no more) in all
that can make existence happy and noble, may be a dream,
and Mr. Harrison may be right in calling it so. In de-
riding it he cannot be right. "The eternity of the tabor"
he calls it! Has he never felt, or, at any rate, is he not
able to conceive, a thrill of pleasure at a sympathetic in-
terchange of look, or word, or touch, with a fellow-crea-
ture kind and noble and brilliant, and engaged in the
exhibition of those qualities of heart and intellect which
make him what he is? Multiply and sustain this—suppose yourself surrounded by beings with whom this in-
terchange of sympathy is warm and perpetual. Intensify
it. Increase indefinitely the excellence of one of those
beings, the wonderful and attractive character of his
operations, our own capacities of affection and intellect,
the vividness of our conception, the breadth and firmness of
of our mental grasp, the sharp vigour of our admiration; and,
to exclude satiety, imagine if you like that the operations
which we contemplate and our relations to our companions
are infinitely varied—a supposition for which the size of
the known and unknown universe affords indefinite scope
—or otherwise suppose that sameness ceases to tire, as the
old Greek philosopher thought it might do if we were
better than we are (μεταβολή πάντων γλυκύτατον διὰ πονηρίαν
τινά), or as it would do, I suppose, if we had no memory
of the immediate past. Imagine all this as the very least
that may be hoped, if our own powers of conception are
as slight in respect to the nature of what is to be as our

bodies are in relation to the physical universe. And remember that, if practical duties are necessary for the perfection of life, the universe is not so small but that in some corner of it its Creator might always find something to do for the army of intelligences whom he has thus formed and exalted.

All this, I repeat, may be a dream, but to characterize it as "the eternity of the tabor" shows surely a feebleness of conception or carelessness of representation more worthy of a ready writer than of a serious thinker. And to place before us as a rival conception the fact that some of our good deeds will have indefinite consequences—to call this scanty and fading chain of effects, which we shall be as unable to perceive or control as we have been unable to anticipate—to call this a "posthumous activity," "an eternity of spiritual influence," and a "life beyond the grave," and finally, under the appellation of "incorporation into the glorious future of our race," to claim for it a dignity and value parallel to that which would attach to the Christian's expectation (if solid) of a sensible life of exalted happiness for himself and all good men, is surely nothing more or less than extravagance founded on misnomer.

With regard to the promised incorporation, I should really like to know what is the exact process, or event, or condition, which Mr. Harrison considers himself to understand by the incorporation of a *consensus* of faculties with a glorious future; and whether he arrived at its apprehension by way of "positive knowledge," or by way of "scientific logic."

Mr. Harrison's future life is disposed of by Professor Huxley in a few words: "Throw a stone into the sea, and there is a sense in which it is true that the wavelets which spread around it have an effect through all space and time. Shall we say that the stone has a future life?"

To this I only add the question whether I am not justified in saying that Mr. Harrison does not adequately distinguish between the nature of a fiddle and the nature of a tune, and would contend (if consistent) that a violin which had been burnt to ashes would, notwithstanding, continue to exist, at least as long as a tune which had been played upon it survived in the memory of any one who had heard it—the *consensus* of its capacities being, it would seem, incorporated into the glorious future of music.

HON. RODEN NOEL.

DEATH is a phenomenon; but are we phenomena? The question of immortality seems, philosophically speaking, very much to resolve itself into that of personality. Are we persons, spirits, or are we things? Perhaps we are a loose collection of successive qualities? That seems to be the latest conclusion of positive and Agnostic biological philosophy. The happy thought 'which, as Dr.

Stirling suggests, was probably thrown out in a spirit of persiflage by Hume has been adopted in all seriousness by his followers. Mr. Harrison is very bitter with those who want to explain mental and moral phenomena by physiology. But, as Prof. Huxley remarks, he seems in many parts of his essay to do the same thing himself. What could Büchner, or Carl Vogt, say stronger than this ? "At last, the prick of a needle, or a grain of mineral, will in an instant lay to rest forever man's body and its unity, and all the spontaneous activities of intelligence, feeling, and action, *with which that compound organism was charged.*" Again, he says, the spiritual faculties are " directly dependent on physical organs "—" stand forth as functions of living organs in given conditions of the organism." Again : " At last the man Newton dies, that is, the body is dispersed into gas and dust." Mr. Harrison, then, though a positivist, bound to know only successive phenomena, seems to know the body as a material entity possessed of such functions as conscience, reason, imagination, perception—to know that Newton's body thought out the " Principia," and Shakespeare's conceived " Hamlet." Indeed, Agnosticism generally, though with a show of humility, seems rather arbitrary in its selection of what we shall know, and what we shall not; we must know something; so we shall know that we have ideas and feelings, but not the personal identity that alone makes them intelligible, or we shall use the word, and yet speak as if the idea were a figment; we shall know qualities, but not substance ; " functions " and " forces," but not the some one or something of which they must be functions and forces to be conceivable at all.   Yet *naturam expellas furca*, etc. Common-sense insists on retaining the fundamental laws of human thought, not being able to get rid of them ; and hence the hap-hazard, instead of systematic and orderly, fashion in which the new philosophy deals with universal convictions, denying even that they exist out of theology and *métaphysique.*

Thus (in apparent contradiction to the statements quoted), we are told that it is " man who loves, thinks, acts ; not the ganglia, or sinuses, or any organ" that does so.   But perhaps the essayist means that all the body together does so.   He says a man is "the consensus, or combined activity of his faculties."   What is meant by this phraseology ?   It is just this " *his,*" this " *consensus,*" or " *combined* acting," that is inconceivable without the focus of unity, in which many contemporaneous phenomena, and many past and present, meet to be compared, remembered, identified, as belonging to the same self ; so only can they be known phenomena at all. Well, do we find in examining the physical structure of man's body as solid, heavy, extended, devisible, or its living organs and their physical functions, or the rearrangement of molecules of carbon, nitrogen, hydrogen, etc., into living tissue, or its oxidation, anything corresponding to the consciousness of personal moral agency, and personal identity ? . We put the two classes of conception side by side, and they seem to refuse to be identified—man as one and the same conscious moral agent—and his body, or the bumps on his skull; or is man indeed a function of his own body? Are we right in talking of our bodies as material things, and of ourselves as if we were not things, but persons with mights, rights, and duties? We ought, perhaps, to talk—theologies and philosophies being now exploded—not of our having bodies, but of bodies having us, and of bodies having rights or duties. Perhaps Dundreary was mistaken, and the tail may wag the dog after all.

Mr. Harrison says: "Orthodoxy has so long been accustomed to take itself for granted, that we are apt to forget how very short a period of human history this sublimated essence" (the immaterial soul) "has been current. There is not a trace of it in the Bible in its present sense." This reminds one rather of Mr. Matthew Arnold's contention that the Jews did not believe in God. But really it does not much signify what particular intellectual theories have been entertained by different men at different times about the nature of God or of the soul: the question is whether you do not find on the whole among them all a consciousness or conviction that there is a Higher Being above them, together with a power of distinguishing themselves from their own bodies, and the world around them—in consequence of this, too, a belief in personal immortality. Many in all ages believe that the dead have spoken to us from beyond the grave. But into that I will not enter. *Are we our bodies?* that seems to be the point. Now, I do not think positivism has any right to assume that we are, even on its own principles and professions.

Mr. Harrison has a very forcible passage, in which
he enlarges upon this theme : that "the laws of the
separate functions of body, mind, or feeling, have
visible relations to each other; are inextricably woven in
with each other, act and react. . . . From the summit of
spiritual life to the base of corporeal life, whether we pass
up or down the gamut of human forces, there runs one
organic correlation and sympathy of parts. Touch the
smallest fibre in the corporeal man, and in some infinitesimal way we may watch the effect in the moral man.
When we rouse chords of the most glorious ecstasy of the
soul, we may see the vibrations of them visibly thrilling
upon the skin." Here we are in the region of positive
facts as specially made manifest by recent investigation.
And the orthodox schools need to recognize the significance of such facts. The close interdependence of body
and soul is a startling verity that must be looked in the
face ; and the discovery has, no doubt, gone far to shake
the faith of many in human immortality, as well as in
other momentous kindred truths. It has been so with myself.
But I think the old dictum of Bacon about the effect of
a little and more knowledge will be found applicable
after all. Let us look these facts very steadily in the
face. When we have thought for a long time, there is a
feeling of pain in the head. That is a feeling, observe, in
our own conscious selves. Further, by observation and
experiment, it has been made certain that some molecular
change in the nervous substance of the brain (to the
renewal of which oxygenated blood is necessary) is going

on, while the process of thinking takes place—though we are not conscious of it in our own case, except as a matter of inference. The thought itself seems, when we reflect on it, partly due to the action of an external world or cosmos upon us; partly to our own " forms of thought," or fixed ways of perceiving and thinking, which have been ours so long as we can remember, and which do not belong to us more than to other individual members of the human family; again partly to our own past experience. But what *is* this material process accompanying thought, which conceivably we might perceive if we could see the inside of our own bodies? Why it too can only seem what it seems by virtue of our own personal past experience, and our own human as well as individual modes of conceiving. Is not that " positive " too? Will not men of science agree with me that such is the fact? In short, our bodies, on any view of them, *Science herself has taught us*, are *percepts and concepts of ours*—I don't say of the " soul," or the mind, or any *bête noire* of the sort, but of *ourselves*, who surely cannot be altogether *bêtes noires*. They are as much percepts and concepts of ours as is the material world outside them. Are they coloured? Colour, we are told, is a sensation. Are they hard or soft? These are our sensations, and relative to us. The elements of our food enter into relations we name living; their molecules enter into that condition of unstable equilibrium; there is motion of parts fulfilling definite intelligible and constant uses, in some cases subject to our own intelligent direction. But all this is what appears to our intelligence, and it appears different, according to the stages of intelligence at which we arrive; a good deal of it is hypothesis of our own minds. Readers of Berkeley and Kant need not be told this; it is now universally acknowledged by the competent. The atomic theory is a working hypothesis of our minds only. Space and time are relative to our intelligence, to the succession of our thoughts, to our own faculties of motion, motion being also a conception of ours. Our bodies, in fact, as positivists often tells us, and as we now venture to remind *them*, are *phenomena*, that is, *orderly appearances to us*. They further tell us generally that there is nothing which thus appears, or that we cannot know that there is anything beyond the appearance. What, then, according to positivism itself, is the most we are entitled to affirm with regard to the dead? Simply that there are *no appearances to us* of a living personality *in connection with* those phenomena which we call a dead body, any more than there are in connection with the used-up materials of burned tissues that pass by osmosis into the capillaries, and away by excretory ducts. But are we entitled to affirm that the *person* is extinct -- is dissolved—the one conscious self in whom these bodily phenomena centred (except so far as they centred in us), who was the focus of them, gave them form, made them what they were; whose thoughts wandered up and down through eternity; of whom, therefore, the bodily as well as mental and spiritual functions were functions, so far as the body entered into the conscious self at all? We can, on the contrary, only affirm that probably the person no longer perceives, and is conscious, *in connection with this form* we look upon, wherein so-called chemical affinities now prevail altogether over so-called vital power. But even in life the body is always changing and decomposing—foreign substances are always becoming a new body, and the old body becoming a foreign substance. Yet the person remains one and the same. True, positivism tries to eliminate persons, and reduce all to appearances ; but this is too glaring a violation of common-sense, and I do not think from his language Mr. Harrison quite means to do this. Well, by spirit, even by " soul," most people, let me assure him, only mean *our own conscious personal selves.* For myself, indeed, I believe that there cannot be appearances without something to appear. But seeing that the material world is in harmony with our intelligence, and presents all the appearance of intelligent coöperation of parts with a view to ends, I believe, with a great English thinker, whose loss we have to deplore (James Hinton), that all this is the manifestation of life —of living spirits or persons, not of dead, inert matter, though from our own spiritual deadness or inertness it appears to us material. Upon our own moral and spiritual life, in fact, depends the measure of our knowledge and perception. I can indeed admit with Mr. Harrison that probably there must always be to us the phenomenon, the body, the external ; but it may be widely different from what it seems now. We may be made one with the great Elohim, or angels of Nature who create us, or we may still grovel in dead material bodily life. We now appear to ourselves and to others as bodily, as material. Body, and soul or mind, are two opposite phenomenal poles of one reality, which is self or spirit; but though these phenomena may vary, the creative, informing spirit, which underlies all, of which we partake, which is absolute, divine, this can never be destroyed. "In God we live, move, and have our being." It is held, indeed, by the new philosophy, that the temporal, the physical, and the composite (elements of matter and "feeling"), are the basis of our higher consciousness: on the contrary, I hold that this is absurd, and that the one eternal consciousness or spirit must be the basis of the physical, composite, and temporal; is needed to give unity and harmony to the body. One is a little ashamed of agreeing with an old-fashioned thinker, whom an old-fashioned poet pronounced the "first of those who know," that the spirit is organizing vital principle of the body, not *vice versa*. The great difficulty, no doubt, is that apparent irruption of the external into the personal, when, as the essayist says, "impair a man's secretions, and moral sense is dulled, discoloured, depraved." But it is our spiritual deadness that has put us into this physical condition; and probably it is *we* who are responsible in a fuller sense than we can realize now for this effect upon us, which must be in the end too for purposes of discipline; it belongs to our spiritual history and purpose. Moreover, this external world is not so foreign to us as we imagine; it is spiritual, and between all spirit there is solidarity.

Mr. Hinton observes (and here I agree with him rather than with Mr. Harrison) that the defect and falseness of our knowing must be in the knowing by only part of ourselves. Whereas sense had to be supplemented by intellect, and proved misleading without it, so intellect, even in the region of knowledge, has to be supplemented by moral sense, which is the highest faculty in us. We are at present misled by a false view of the world, based on sense and intellect only. Death is but a hideous illusion of our deadness—

> "Death is the veil which those who live call life :
> We sleep and it is lifted.".

The true definition of the actual is that which is true for, which satisfies the whole being of humanity. We must ask of a doctrine, " Does it answer in the moral region ?" if so, it is as true as we can have it with our present knowledge; but, if the moral experiment fails, it is not true. Conscience has the highest authority about knowledge, as it has about conduct. Now apply this to the negations of positivism, and the belief Comte would substitute for faith in God, and personal immortality. Kant sufficiently proved that these are postulates required by Practical Reason, and on this ground he believed them. I am not blind to the beauty and nobleness of Comte's moral ideal (not without debt to Christ's as expounded) by himself, and here by Mr. Harrison. Still I say, The moral experiment fails. Some of us may seek to benefit the world, and then desire rest. But what of the maimed and broken and aimless lives around us ? What

of those we have lost, who were dearer to us than our own
selves, full of fairest hope and promise, unaware annihilated in earliest dawn, whose dewy bud yet slept unfolded ?
If they were *things*, doubtless we *might* count them às
so much manure, in which to grow those still more
beautiful though still brief-flowering human aloes, which
positivism, though knowing nothing but present phenomena, and denying God, is able confidently to promise us
in some remote future. But alas! they *seemed* living
spirits, able to hope for infinite love, progressive virtue,
the beatific vision of God himself! And they really
were—so much manure ! Why, as has already been asked,
are such ephemerals worth living for, however many of
them there may be, whose lives are as an idle flash in the
pan, always promising, yet failing to attain any substantial or enduring good ? What of these agonizing
women and children, now the victims of Ottoman blood-
madness ? What of all the cramped, unlovely, debased,
or slow-tortured yet evanescent lives of myriads in our
great cities ? These cannot have the philosophic aspirations of culture. They have too often none at all. Go
proclaim to them this gospel, supplementing it by the
warning that in the end there will remain only a huge
block of ice in a " wide, gray, lampless, deep, unpeopled
world !" I could believe in the pessimism of Schopenhauer, not in this jaunty optimism of Comte.

Are we then indeed orphans ? Will the tyrant go ever
unpunished, the wrong ever unredressed, the poor and
helpless remain always trampled and unhappy ? Must the

battle of good and evil in ourselves and others hang always trembling in the balance, forever undecided ; or does it all mean nothing more than we see now, and is the glorious world but some ghastly illusion of insanity? When "the fever called living is over at last," is all indeed over? Thank God that through this Babel of discordant voices modern men can still hear His accents who said, "Come unto me, all ye that are weary and are heavy laden, and I will give you rest."

LORD SELBORNE.

I AM too well satisfied with Lord Blachford's paper to think that I can add anything of importance to it. The little I would say has reference to our actual knowledge of the soul during this life—meaning by the soul what Lord Blachford means, viz., the conscious being which each man calls "himself."

It appears to me that what we know and can observe tends to confirm the testimony of our consciousness to the reality of the distinction between the body and the soul. From the necessity of the case, we cannot observe any manifestations of the soul except during the time of its association with the body. This limit of our experience applies, not to the "ego" of which alone each man has any direct knowledge, but to the perceptible indication of consciousness in others. It is impossible, in the nature of things, that any man can ever have had experience of the total cessation of his own consciousness; and the idea of such a cessation is much less natural and much more difficult to realize than that of its continuance. We observe the phenomena of death in others, and infer, by irresistible induction, that the same thing will also happen to ourselves. But these phenomena carry us only to the dissociation of the "ego" from the body, not to its extinction.

Nothing else can be credible if our consciousness is not; and I have said that this bears testimony to the reality of the distinction between soul and body. Each man is conscious of using his own body as an instrument, in the same sense in which he would use any other machine. He passes a different moral judgment on the mechanical and involuntary actions of his body, from that which he feels to be due to its actions resulting from his own free-will. The unity and identity of the "ego," from the beginning to the end of life, is of the essence of his consciousness.

In accordance with this testimony are such facts as the following: that the body has no proper unity, identity, or continuity, through the whole of life—all its constituent parts being in a constant state of flux and change; that many parts and organs of the body may be removed with no greater effect upon the "ego" than when we take off any article of clothing; and that those organs which cannot be removed or stopped in their action without death are distributed over different parts of the body, and are homogeneous in their material and structure with others which we can lose without the sense that any change has passed over our proper selves. If, on the one hand, a diseased state of some bodily organs interrupts the reasonable manifestations of the soul through the body, the cases are, on the other, not rare in which the whole body decays and falls into extreme age, weakness, and even decrepitude, while vigour, freshness, and youthfulness, are characteristic of the mind.

The attempt, in Butler's work, to reason from the indivisibility and indestructibility of the soul as ascertained facts, is less satisfactory than most of that great writer's arguments, which are generally rather intended to be destructive of objections than demonstrative of positive truths. But the modern scientific doctrine, that all matter and all force are indestructible, is not without interest in relation to that argument. There must at least be a natural presumption from that doctrine that, if the soul during life has a real existence distinct from the body, it is not annihilated by death. If, indeed, it were a mere " force " (such as heat, light, etc., are supposed by modern philosophers to be—though men who are not philosophers may be excused if they find some difficulty in understanding exactly what is meant by the term when so used), it would be consistent with that doctrine that the soul might be transmuted after death into some other form of force. But the idea of " force " in this sense (whatever may be its exact meaning) seems wholly inapplicable to the conscious being which a man calls "himself."

The resemblances in the nature and organization of animal and vegetable bodies seem to me to confirm, instead of weakening, the impression that the body of man is a machine under the government of the soul, and quite distinct from it. Plants manifest no consciousness; all our knowledge of them tends irresistibly to the conclusion that there is in them no intelligent, much less any reasonable, principle of life. Yet they are machines very like the human body; not, indeed, in their formal development or their exact chemical processes, but in the general scheme and functions of their organism—in their laws of nutrition, digestion, assimilation, respiration, and especially reproduction. They are bodies without souls, living a physical life, and subject to a physical death. The inferior animals have bodies still more like our own; indeed in their higher orders, resembling them very closely indeed; and they have also a principle of life quite different from that of plants, with various degrees of consciousness, intelligence, and volition. Even in their principle of life, arguments founded on observation and comparison (though not on individual consciousness), more or less similar to those which apply to man, tend to show that there is something distinct from, and more than, the body. But, of all these inferior animals, the intelligence differs from that of man, not in degree only, but in kind. Nature is their simple, uniform, and sufficient law; their very arts (which are often wonderful) come to them by

Nature, except when they are trained by man ; there is
in them no sign of discourse, of reason, of morality, or of
the knowledge of good and evil.   The very similarity of
their bodily structure to that of man tends, when these
differences are noted, to add weight to the other natural
evidence of the distinctness of man's soul from his body.

The immortality of the soul seems to me to be one of
those truths for the belief in which, when authoritatively
declared, man is prepared by the very constitution of his
nature.

CANON BARRY.

A NY one who from the ancient position of Christianity
looks on the controversy between Mr. Harrison and
Prof. Huxley on " The Soul and Future Life " (to which I
propose mainly to confine myself) will be tempted with
Faulconbridge to observe, not without a touch of grim
satisfaction, how, " from north to south, Austria and
France shoot in each other's mouth."   The fight is fierce
enough to make him ask, *Tantœne animis sapientibus irœ?*
But he will see that each is far more effective in battering
the lines of the enemy than in strengthening his own.
Nor will he be greatly concerned if both from time to
time lodge a shot or two in the battlements on which he
stands, with some beating of that " drum scientific "
which seems to me to be in these days always as resonant,

8

sometimes with as much result of merely empty sound, as " the drum ecclesiastic," against which Prof. Huxley is so fond of warning us. Those whom Mr. Harrison calls " theologians," and whom Prof. Huxley less appropriately terms " priests " (for of priesthood there is here no question), may indeed think that, if the formidable character of an opponent's position is to be measured by the scorn and fury with which it is assailed, their ground must be strong indeed; and they will possibly remember an old description of a basis less artificial than " pulpit-stairs," from which men may look without much alarm, while " the floods come and the winds blow." Gaining from this conviction courage to look more closely, they will perceive, as I have said, that each of the combatants is far stronger on the destructive than on the constructive side.

Mr. Harrison's earnest and eloquent plea against the materialism which virtually, if not theoretically, makes all that we call spirit a mere function of material organization (like the ἁρμονία of the " Phædo "), and against the exclusive " scientism " which, because it cannot find certain entities along its line of investigation, asserts loudly that they are either non-existent or " unknowable," is strong, and (*pace* Prof. Huxley) needful; not, indeed, against him (for he knows better than to despise the metaphysics in which he is so great an adept), but against many adherents, prominent rather than eminent, of the school in which he is a master. Nor is its force destroyed by exposing, however keenly and sarcastically, some inconsistencies of argument, not inaptly corresponding (as it seems to me) with similar inconsistencies in the popular exposition of the views which it attacks. If Prof. Huxley is right (as surely he is) in pleading for perfect freedom and boldness in the investigation of the phenomena of humanity from the physical side, the counter-plea is equally irresistible for the value of an independent philosophy of mind, starting from the metaphysical pole of thought, and reasoning positively on the phenomena which, though they may have many connections with physical laws, are utterly inexplicable by them. We might, indeed, demur to his inference that the discovery of "antecedence in the molecular fact" necessarily leads to a "physical theory of moral phenomena," and *vice versa*, as savouring a little of the *post hoc, ergo propter hoc*. Inseparable connection it would imply; but the ultimate causation might lie in something far deeper, underlying both "the molecular" and "the spiritual fact." But still to establish such antecedence would be an · important scientific step, and the attempt might· be made from either side.

On the other hand, Prof. Huxley's trenchant attack on the unreality of the positivist assumption of a right to take names which in the old religion at least mean something firm and solid, and to sublime them into the cloudy forms of transcendental theory, and on the arbitrary application of the word "selfishness," with all its degrading associations, to the consciousness of personality here and the hope of a nobler personality in the future, leaves nothing to be desired. I fear that his friends the priests

would be accused of the crowning sin of " ecclesiasticism "
(whatever that may be) if they used denunciations half
so sharp.   Except with a few sarcasms which he cannot
resist the temptation of flinging at them by the way, they
will have nothing with which to quarrel; and possibly
they may even learn from him to consider these as claps
of · " cheap thunder " from the " pulpit," in that old
sense of the word in which it designates the professorial
chair.

The whole of Mr. Harrison's two papers may be resolved
into an attack on the true individuality of man, first on
the speculative, then on the moral side; from the one
point of view denouncing the belief in it as a delusion,
from the other branding the desire of it as a moral
degradation.   The connection of the two arguments is
instructive and philosophical.   For no argument merely
speculative, ignoring all moral considerations, will really
be listened to.   His view of the soul as " a consensus of
human faculties " reminds us curiously of the Buddhist
" groups;" his description of a " perpetuity of sensation as
the true hell " breathes the very spirit of the longing for
Nirvana.   Both he and his Asiatic predecessors are certainly right in considering the " delusion of individual
existence " as the chief delusion to be got rid of on the
way to a perfect Agnosticism, in respect of all that is not
merely phenomenal.   It is true that he protests in terms
against a naked materialism, ignoring all spiritual phenomena as having a distinctive character of their own ; but
yet, when he tells us that " to talk about a bodiless being

thinking and loving is simply to talk of the thoughts and feelings of Nothing," he certainly appears to assume substantially the position of the materialism he denounces, which (as has been already said) holds these spiritual energies to be merely results of the bodily organization, as the excitation of an electric current is the result of the juxtaposition of certain material substances. If a bodiless being is Nothing, there can be no such thing as an intrinsic or independent spiritual life; and it is difficult for ordinary minds to attach any distinct meaning to the declaration that the soul is "a conscious unity of being," if that being depends on an organization which is unquestionably discerptible, and of which (as Butler remarks) large parts may·be lost without affecting this consciousness of personality.

Now this is, after all, the only point worth fighting about. Mr. Hutton has already said with perfect truth that by "the soul" we mean that "which lies at the bottom of the sense of personal identity—the thread of the continuity running through all our checkered life," and which remains unbroken amidst the constant flux of change both in our material body, and in the circumstances of our material life. This belief is wholly independent of any "metaphysical hypothesis" of modern "orthodoxy," whether it is, or is not, rightly described as a "juggle of ideas," and of any examination of the question (on which Lord Blachford has touched) whether, if it seem such to "those trained in positive habits of thought," the fault lies in it or in them. I may remark,

in passing, that in this broad and simple sense it certainly
runs through the whole Bible, and has much that is "akin
to it in the Old Testament." For even in the darkest
and most shadowy ideas of the *Sheôl* of the other world,
the belief in a true personal identity is taken absolutely
for granted; and it is not a little curious to notice how in
the Book of Job the substitution for it of "an immortality in the race" (although there, not in the whole of
humanity, but simply in the tribe or family) is offered,
and rejected as utterly insufficient to satisfy either the
speculation of the intellect or the moral demands of the
conscience.[1] Now is it not worth while to protest against
the caricature of this belief, as a belief in "man plus a
hetereogeneous entity" called the soul, which can be only
intended as a sarcasm. But we cannot acquiesce in any
statement which represents the belief in this immaterial
and indivisible personality as resting simply on the notion that it is needed to explain the acts of the human
organism. For, as a matter of fact, those who believe in
it conceive it to be declared by a direct consciousness, the
most simple and ultimate of all acts of consciousness.
They hold this consciousness of a personal identity and
individuality, unchanging amid material change, to be
embodied in all the language and literature of man; and
they point to the inconsistencies in the very words of
those who argue against it, as proofs that man cannot
divest himself of it. No doubt they believe that so the
acts of the organism are best explained, but it is not on the

---

1 *See* Job, xiv. 21, 22.

necessity of such explanation that they base their belief, and this fact separates altogether their belief in the human soul, as an immaterial entity, from those conceptions of a soul, in animal, vegetable, or even inorganic substances, with which Mr. Harrison insists on confounding it. Of the true character of animal nature we know nothing (although we may conjecture much), just because we have not in regard to it the direct consciousness which we have in regard to our own nature. Accordingly, we need not trouble our argument for a soul in man with any speculation as to a true soul in the brute creatures.

In what relation this personality stands to the particles which at any moment compose the body, and which are certainly in a continual state of flux, or to the law of structure which in living beings, by some power to us unknown, assimilates these particles, is a totally different question. I fear that Mr. Harrison will be displeased with me if I call it "a mystery." But, whatever future advances of science may do for us in the matter—and I hope they may do much—I am afraid I must still say that this relation is a mystery which has been at different times imperfectly represented, both by formal theories and by metaphors, all of which by the very nature of language are connected with original physical conceptions. Let it be granted freely that the progress of modern physiological science has rendered obsolete the old idea that the various organs of the body stand to the true personal being in a purely instrumental relation, such as (for example) is described by Butler in his "Analogy," in the celebrated chapter on "The Future Life." The power of physical influences acting upon the body to affect the energies of thought and will is unquestionable. The belief that the action of all these energies is associated with the molecular change is, to say the least, highly probable. And I may remark that Christianity has no quarrel with these discoveries of modern science; for its doctrine is that for the perfection of man's being a bodily organization is necessary, and that the " intermediate state " is a state of suspense and imperfection, out of which at the word of the Creator, the indestructible personality of man shall rise, to assimilate to itself a glorified body. The doctrine of the resurrection of the body boldly faces the perplexity as to the connection of a body with personality, which so greatly troubled ancient speculation on the immortality of the soul. In respect of the intermediate "state," it only extends (I grant immeasurably) the experience of those suspensions of the will and the full consciousness of personality which we have in life, in sleep, swoon, stupor, dependent on normal and abnormal conditions of the bodily organization; and in respect of the resurrection, it similarly extends the action of that mysterious creative will which moulds the human body of the present life slowly and gradually out of the mere germ, and forms with marvellous rapidity and exuberance of prolific power, lower organisms of high perfection and beauty.

But while modern science teaches us to recognize the influence of the bodily organization on mental energy, it has, with at least equal clearness, brought out in compensation the distinct power of that mental energy, acting by a process wholly different from the chain of physical causation, to alter functionally, and even organically, the bodily frame itself. The Platonic Socrates (it will be remembered) dwells on the power of the spirit to control bodily appetite and even passion (τό θυμοειδές), as also on its having the power to assume qualities, as a proof that it is more ἁρμονία. Surely modern science has greatly strengthened the former part of his argument, by these discoveries of the power of mind over even the material of the body. This is strikingly illustrated (for example to the physician, both by the morbid phenomena of what is called "hysteria," in which the belief in the existence of physical disease actually produces the most remarkable physical effects on the body; and also by the more natural action of the mind on the body, when in sickness a resolution to get well masters the force of disease, or a desire to die slowly fulfils itself. Perhaps even more extraordinary is the fact (I believe sufficiently ascertained) that during pregnancy the presentation of ideas to the mind of the mother actually affects the physical organization of the offspring. Hence I cannot but think that, at least as distinctly as ever, our fuller experience discloses to us two different processes of causation acting upon our complex humanity—the one wholly physical, acting sometimes by the coarser mechanical agencies, sometimes by the subtiler physiological agencies, and in both cases connecting man through the

body with the great laws ruling the physical universe—
the other wholly metaphysical, acting by the simple presentation of ideas to the mind (which may, indeed, be so
purely subjective that they correspond to no objective
reality whatever), and through them, secondarily acting
upon the body, producing, no doubt, the molecular
changes in the brain and the affections of the nervous
tissue which accompany and exhibit mental emotion.
In the normal condition of the earthly life, these two
powers act and react upon each other, neither being absolutely independent of the other. In the perfect state of
the hereafter we believe that it shall be so still. But we
do know of cases in which the metaphysical power is
apparently dormant or destroyed, in which accordingly
all emotions can be produced automatically by physical
processes only, as happens occasionally in dreams
(whether of the day or night), and in morbid conditions,
as of idiocy, which may themselves be produced either by
physical injury or by mental shock. I cannot myself see
any difficulty in conceiving that the metaphysical power
might act, though no doubt in a way of which we have
no present experience, and (according to the Christian
doctrine) in a condition of some imperfection, when the
bodily organization is either suspended or removed. For
to me it seems clear that there is something existent,
which is neither material nor even dependent on material organization. Whether it be stigmatized as a " heterogeneous entity," or graciously designated by the " good
old word soul," is a matter of great indifference. There,

it is ; and if it is, I cannot see why it is inconceivable that it should survive all material change. For here, as in other cases, there seems to be a frequent confusion between conceiving that a thing may be, and conceiving how it may be. Of course, we cannot figure to ourselves the method of the action of a spiritual energy apart from a bodily organization ; in the attempt to do so the mind glides into quasi-corporeal conceptions and expressions, which are a fair mark for satire. But that there may be such action is to me far less inconceivable than that the mere fact of the dissolution of what is purely physical should draw with it the destruction of a soul that can think, love and pray.

I do not think it necessary to dwell at any length on the second of Mr. Harrison's propositions, denouncing the desire of personal and individual existence as "selfishness," with a vigour quite worthy of his royal Prussian model. But history, after all, has recognized that the poor grenadiers had something to say for themselves. Mr. Hutton has already suggested that, if Mr. Harrison had studied the Christian conception of the future life, he could not have written some of his most startling passages, and has protested against the misapplication of the word " selfishness," which in this, as in other controversies, quietly begs the question proposed for discussion. The fact is, that this theory of " altruism," so eloquently set forth by Mr. Harrison and others of his school, simply contradicts human nature, not in its weaknesses or sins, but in its essential characteristics. It is certainly not the weakest or ignoblest of human souls who have felt, at the times of deepest thought and feeling, conscious of but two existences—their own and the Supreme Existence, whether they call it Nature, Law or God. Surely this humanity is a very unworthy deity, at once a vague and shadowy abstraction, and so far as it can be distinctly conceived, like some many-headed idol, magnifying the evil and hideousness as well as the good and beauty of the individual nature. But if it were not so still that individuality, as well as unity, is the law of human nature, is singularly indicated by the very nature of our mental operations. In the study and perception of truth, each man, though he may be guided to it by others, stands absolutely alone; in love, on the other hand, he loses all but the sense of unity; while the conscience holds the balance, recognizing at once individuality and unity. Indeed, the sacredness of individuality is so guarded by the darkness which hides each soul from all perfect knowledge of man, so deeply impressed on the mind by the consciousness of independent thought and will, and on the soul by the sense of incommunicable responsibility, that it cannot merge itself in the life of the race. Self-sacrifice or unselfishness is the conscious sacrifice, not of our own individuality, but of that which seems to minister to it, for the sake of others. The law of human nature, moreover, is such that the very attempt at such sacrifice inevitably strengthens the spiritual individuality in all that makes it worth having. To talk of " a perpetuity of sensation as a true hell " in a being supposed capable of indefinite growth in wisdom, righteousness, and love, is surely to use words which have no intelligible meaning.

No doubt, if we are to take as our guiding principle either altruism or what is rightly designated " selfishness," we must infinitely prefer the former. But where is the necessity ? No doubt the task of harmonizing the two is difficult. But all things worth doing are difficult ; and it might be worth while to consider whether there is not something in the old belief which finds the key to this difficult problem in the consciousness of the relation to One Supreme Being, and, recognizing both the love of man and the love of self, bids them both agree in conscious subordination to a higher love of God. What makes our life here will, we believe, make it up hereafter, only in a purer and nobler form. On earth we live at once in our own individuality and in the life of others. Our heaven is not the extinction of either element of that life—either of individuality, as Mr. Harrison would have it, or of the life in others, as in that idea of a selfish immortality which he has, I think, set up in order to denounce it— but the continued harmony of both under an infinitely increased power of that supreme principle.

MR. W. R. GREG.

IT would seem impossible for Mr. Harrison to write anything that is not stamped with a vigour and racy eloquence peculiarly his own; and the paper which has opened the present discussion is probably far the finest he has given to the world. There is a lofty tone in its imaginative passages which strikes us as unique among negationists, and a vein of what is almost tenderness pervading them, which was not observed in his previous writings. The two combined render the second portion one of the most touching and impressive speculations we have read. Unfortunately, however, Mr. Harrison's innate energy is apt to boil over into a vehemence approaching the intemperate; and the antagonistic atmosphere is so native to his spirit that he can scarcely enter the lists of controversy without an irresistible tendency to become aggressive and unjust; and he is too inclined to forget the first duty of the chivalric militant logician—namely, to select the adversary you assail from the nobler and not the lower form and rank of the doctrine in dispute. The inconsistencies and weaknesses into which this neglect has betrayed him in the instance before us have, however, been so severely dealt with by Mr. Hutton and Prof. Huxley, that I wish rather to direct attention to two or three points of his argument that might otherwise be in danger of escaping the appreciation and gratitude they may fairly claim.

We owe him something, it appears to me, for having inaugurated a discussion which has stirred so many minds to give us on such a question so much' interesting and profound, and more especially so much suggestive, thought. We owe him much, too, because, in dealing with a thesis which it is specially the temptation and the • practice to handle as a theme for declamation, he has so written as to force his antagonists to treat it argumentatively and searchingly as well. Some gratitude, moreover, is due to the man who had the moral courage boldly to avow his adhesion to the negative view when that view is not only in the highest degree unpopular, but is regarded for the most part as condemnable into the bargain, and when, besides, it can scarcely fail to be painful to every man of vivid imagination and of strong affections. It is to his credit also, I venture to think, that, holding this view, he has put it forward, not as an opinion or speculation, but as a settled and deliberate conviction, maintainable by distinct and reputable reasonings, and to be controverted only by pleas analogous in character. For if there be a topic within the wide range of human questioning in reference to which tampering with mental integrity might seem at first sight pardonable, it is that of a future and continued existence. If belief be ever permissible—perhaps I ought to say, if belief be ever possible—on the ground that "there is peace and joy in believing," it is here, where the issues are so vast, where the conception in its highest form is so ennobling, where the practical influences of the Creed are, in

appearance at least, so beneficent. But faith thus arrived
at has ever clinging to it the curse belonging to all ille-
gitimate possessions. It is precarious, because the flaw
in its title-deeds, barely suspected perhaps and never
acknowledged, may any moment be discovered; misgivings
crop up most surely in those hard and gloomy crises of
our lives when unflinching confidence is most essential to
our peace; and the fairy fabric, built up not on grounded
conviction but on craving need, crumbles into dust, and
leaves the spirit with no solid sustenance to rest upon.

Unconsciously, and by implication, Mr. Harrison bears
a testimony he little intended, not, indeed, to the future
existence he denies, but to the irresistible longing and necessity for the very belief he labours to destroy. Perhaps
no writer has more undesignedly betrayed his conviction
that men will not and cannot be expected to surrender
their faith and hope without at least something like a
compensation; certainly no one has ever toiled with more
noble rhetoric to gild and illuminate the substitute with
which he would fain persuade us to rest satisfied. The
nearly universal craving for posthumous existence and
enduring consciousness, which he depreciates with so
harsh a scorn, and which he will not accept as offering
even the shadow or *simulacrum* of an argument for the
Creed, he yet respects enough to recognize that it has its
foundation deep in the framework of our being, that it
cannot be silenced, and may not be ignored. Having no
precious metal to pay it with, he issues paper-money instead, skilfully engraved and gorgeously gilded to look

as like the real coin as may be. It is in vain to deny that there is something touching and elevating in the glowing eloquence with which he paints the picture of lives devoted to efforts in the service of the race, spent in labouring, each of us in his own sphere, to bring about the grand ideal he fancies for humanity, and drawing strength and reward for long years of toil in the anticipation of what man will be when those noble dreams shall have been realized at last—even though we shall never see what we have wrought so hard to win. It is vain to deny, moreover, that these dreams appear more solid and less wild or vague when we remember how close an analogy we may detect in the labours of thousands around us who spend their whole career on earth in building up, by sacrifice and painful struggles, wealth, station, fame, and character, for their children, whose enjoyment of these possessions they will never live to witness, without their passionate zeal in the pursuit being in any way cooled by the discouraging reflection. Does not this oblige us to confess that the posthumous existence Mr. Harrison describes is not altogether an airy fiction? Still, somehow, after a few moments spent in the thin atmosphere into which his brilliant language and unselfish imagination have combined to raise us, we— ninety-nine out of every hundred of us at the least—sink back breathless and wearied after the unaccustomed soaring amid light so dim, and craving, as of yore, after something more personal, more solid, and more *certain*.

To that more solid certainty I am obliged vto confess,

9

sorrowfully and with bitter disappointment, that I can contribute nothing—nothing, I mean, that resembles evidence, that can properly be called argument, or that I can hope will be received as even the barest confirmation. Alas! *can* the wisest and most sanguine of us all bring anything beyond our own personal sentiments to swell the common hope? We have aspirations to multiply, but who has any *knowledge* to enrich our store? I have of course read most of the pleadings in favour of the ordinary doctrine of the future state; naturally also, in common with all graver natures, I have meditated yet more; but these pleadings, for the most part, sound to anxious ears little else than the passionate outcries of souls that cannot endure to part with hopes on which they have been nurtured, and which are entertwined with their tenderest affections. Logical reasons to *compel* conviction, I have met with none—even from the interlocutors in this actual Symposium. Yet few can have sought for such more yearningly. I may say I share in the anticipations of believers; but I share them as aspirations, sometimes approaching almost to a faith, occasionally, and for a few moments, perhaps rising into something like a trust, but never able to settle into the consistency of a definite and enduring creed. I do not know how far even this incomplete state of mind may not be merely the residuum of early upbringing and habitual associations. But I must be true to my darkness as courageously as to my light. I cannot rest in comfort on arguments that to my spirit have no cogency, nor can I pretend to respect or be content with reasons which carry no penetrating conviction along with them. I will not make buttresses do the work or assume the posture of foundations. I will not cry " Peace, peace, when there is no peace." I have said elsewhere, and at various epochs of life, why the ordinary " proofs " confidently put forward and gorgeously arrayed " have no help in them; " while, nevertheless, the pictures which imagination depicts are so inexpressibly alluring. The more I think and question, the more do doubts and difficulties crowd around my horizon, and cloud over my sky. Thus it is that I am unable to bring aid or sustainment to minds as troubled as my own, and perhaps less willing to admit that the great enigma is, and must remain, insoluble. Of two things, however, I feel satisfied—that the negative doctrine is no more susceptible of proof than the affirmative, and that our opinion, be it only honest can have no influence whatever on the issue, nor upon its bearing on ourselves.

Two considerations that have been borne in upon my mind while following this controversy may be worth mentioning, though neither can be called exactly helpful. One is, that we find the most confident, unquestioning, dogmatic belief in heaven (and its correlative) in those whose heaven is the most unlikely and impossible, the most entirely made up of mundane and material elements, of gorgeous glories and of fading splendours[1]—just such things

---

1 "There may be crowns of material splendour, there may be trees of un-fading loveliness, there may be pavements of emerald, and canopies of the brightest radiance, and gardens of deep and tranquil security, and palaces

as uncultured and undisciplined natures most envied or pined after on earth, such as the lower order of minds could best picture and would naturally be most dazzled by. The higher intelligences of our race, who need a spiritual heaven, find their imaginations fettered by the scientific training which, imperfect though it be, clips their wings in all directions, forbids their glowing fancy, and annuls that gorgeous creation, and bars the way to each successive local habitation that is instinctively wanted to give reality to the ideal they aspire to ; till, in the effort to frame a future existence without a future world, to build up a state of being that shall be worthy of its denizens, and from which everything material shall be excluded, they at last discover that in renouncing the " physical " and inadmissible they have been forced to renounce the " conceivable " as well ; and a dimness and fluctuating uncertainty gathers round a scene from which all that is concrete and definable, and would therefore be incongruous, has been shut out. The next world cannot, it is felt, be a material one ; and a truly " spiritual " one even the saint cannot conceive so as to bring it home to natures still shrouded in the garments of the flesh.

The other suggestion that has occurred to me is this

---

of proud and stately decoration and a city of lofty pinnacles, through which there unceasingly flows a river of gladness, and where jubilee is ever sung by a concord of seraphic voices."—*Dr. Chalmer's Sermons.*

> " Poor fragments all of this low earth—
> Such as in dreams could hardly soothe
> A soul that once had tasted of immortal truth."
>
> *Christian Year.*

It must be conceded that the doctrine of a future life is by no means as universally diffused as it is the habit loosely to assert. It is not always discoverable among primitive and savage races. It existed among pagan nations in a form so vague and hazy as to be describable rather as a dream than a religious faith. It can scarcely be determined whether the Chinese, whose cultivation is perhaps the most ancient existing in the world, can be ranked among distinct believers ; while the conception of *Nirvana*, which prevails in the meditative minds of other Orientals, is more a sort of conscious non-existence than a future life. With the Jews, moreover, as is well known, the belief was not indigenous, but imported, and by no means an early importation. But what is not so generally recognized is that, even among ourselves in these days, the conviction of thoughtful natures varies curiously in strength and in features at different periods of life. In youth, when all our sentiments are most vivacious and dogmatic, most of us not only cling to it as an intellectual creed, but are accustomed to say and feel that, without it as a solace and a hope to rest upon, this world would be stripped of its deepest fascinations. It is from minds of this age, whose vigour is unimpaired and whose relish for the joys of earth is most expansive, that the most glowing delineations of heaven usually proceed, and on whom the thirst for felicity and knowledge, which can be slaked at no earthly fountains, has the most exciting power. Then comes the busy turmoil of our mid-career, when the present curtains off the future from our thoughts, and when a

renewed existence in a different scene is recalled to our
fancy chiefly in crises of bereavement.   And, finally, is it
not the case that in our fading years—when something of
the languor and placidity of age is creeping over us, just
when futurity is coming consciously and rapidly more
near, and when one might naturally expect it to occupy
us more incessantly and with more anxious and searching
glances—we think of it less frequently, believe in it less
confidently, desire it less eagerly, than in our youth?
Such, at least, has been my observation and experience,
especially among the more reflective and inquiring order
of men.   The life of the hour absorbs us most completely,
as the hours grow fewer and less full; the pleasures, the
exemptions, the modest interests, the afternoon peace, the
gentle affections, of the present scene, obscure the
future from our view, and render it, curiously enough,
even less interesting than the past.   To-day, which may
be our last, engrosses us far more than to-morrow, which
may be our FOREVER; and the grave into which we are just
stepping down troubles us far less than in youth, when
half a century lay between us and it.

What is the explanation of this strange phenomenon?
Is it a merciful dispensation arranged by the Ruler of our
life to soften and to ease a crisis which would be too grand
and awful to be faced with dignity or calm, if it were
actually *realized* at all?   Is it that thought—or that vague
substitute for thought which we call time—has brought
us, half unconsciously, to the conclusion that the whole
question is insoluble, and that reflection is wasted where

reflection can bring us no nearer to an issue ? Or, finally, as I know is true far oftener than we fancy, is it that three-score years and ten have quenched the passionate desire for life with which at first we stepped upon the scene? We are tired, some of us, with unending and unprofitable toil ; we are satiated, others of us, with such ample pleasures as earth can yield us; we have had enough of ambition, alike in its successes and its failures; the joys and blessings of human affection on which, whatever their crises and vicissitudes, no righteous or truthful man will cast a slur, are yet so blended with pains which partake of their intensity ; the thirst for knowledge is not slaked, indeed, but the capacity for the labour by which alone it can be gained has consciously died out ; the appetite for life, in short, is gone, the frame is worn and the faculties exhausted ; and —possibly this is the key to the phenomenon we are examining—*age* CANNOT, from the véry law of its nature, *conceive itself endowed with the bounding energies of youth,* and without that vigour, both of exertion and desire, renewed existence can offer no inspiring charms. . Our being upon earth has been enriched by vivid interests and precious joys, and we are deeply grateful for the gift ; but we are wearied with one life, and feel scarcely qualified to enter on the claims, even though balanced by the felicities and glories, of another. It may be the fatigue which comes with age—fatigue of the fancy as well as of the frame ; but, somehow, what we yearn for most instinctively at last is *rest,* and the peace which we can imagine the easiest because we know it best is that of sleep.

Rev. BALDWIN BROWN.

THE theologians appear to have fallen upon evil days. Like some of old, they are filled with rebuke from all sides. They are bidden to be silent, for their day is over. But some things, like nature, are hard to get rid of. Expelled, they "recur" swiftly. Foremost among these is theology. It seems as if nothing could long restrain man from this, the loftiest exercise of his powers. The theologians and the Comtists have met in the sense which Mr. Huxley justly indicates; he is himself working at the foundations of a larger, nobler, and more complete theology. But, for the present, theology suffers affliction, and the theologians have in no small measure themselves to thank for it. The protest rises from all sides, clear and strong, against the narrow, formal, and in these last days, selfish system of thought and expectation, which they have presented as their kingdom of heaven to the world.

I never read Mr. Harrison's brilliant essays, full as they always are of high aspiration and of stimulus to noble endeavour, without finding the judgment which I cannot but pass in my own mind on his unbeliefs and denials, largely tempered by thankfulness. I rejoice in the passionate earnestness with which he lifts the hearts of his readers to ideals which it seems to me that Christianity—that Christianity which as a living force in the apostles' days turned the world upside down, that is, right side up, with its face toward heaven and God—alone can realize for man.

I recall a noble passage written by Mr. Harrison some years ago : "A religion of action, a religion of social duty' devotion to an intelligible and sensible Head, a real sense of incorporation with a living and controlling force, the deliberate effort to serve an immortal Humanity—this, and this alone, can absorb the musings and the cravings of the spiritual man."[1]   It seems to me that it would be difficult for any one to set forth in more weighty and eloquent words the kind of object which Christianity proposes, and the kind of help toward the attainment of the object which the Incarnation affords.   And in the matter now under debate, behind the stern denunciation of the selfish striving toward a personal immortality which Mr. Harrison utters with his accustomed force, there seems to lie not only a yearning for, but a definite vision of, an immortality which shall not be selfish, but largely fruitful to public good.   It is true that, as has been forcibly pointed out, the form which it wears is utterly vain and illusory, and wholly incapable, one would think, of accounting for the enthusiastic eagerness with which it appears to be sought.   May not the eagerness be really kindled by a larger and more far-reaching vision—the Christian vision, which has become obscured to so many faithful servants of duty by the selfishness and vanity with which much that goes by the name of the Christian life in these days has enveloped it ; but which has not ceased and will not cease, in ways which even conscious-

---

ness cannot always trace, to cast its spell on human
hearts ?

Mr. Harrison seems to start in his argument with the
conviction that there is a certain baseness in this longing
for immortality, and he falls on the belief with a fierce-
ness which the sense of its baseness alone could justify.
But surely he must stamp much more with the same
brand. Each day's struggle to live is a bit of the baseness, and there seems to be no answer to Mr. Hutton's remark that the truly unselfish action under such conditions
would be suicide. But, at any rate, it is clear from history that the men who formulated the doctrine and per-
fected the art of suicide in the early days of imperial
Rome belonged to the most basely selfish and heartless
generation that has ever cumbered this sorrowful world.
The love of life is, on the whole, a noble thing, for the
staple of life is duty. The more I see of classes in which,
at first sight, selfishness seems to reign, the more am I
struck with the measure in which duty, thought for others,
and work for others, enters into their lives. The desire
to live on, to those who catch the Christian idea, and
would follow him who " came, not to be ministered unto,
but to minister," is a desire to work on, and by living to
bless more richly a larger circle in a wider world.

I can even cherish some thankfulness for the fling at
the eternity of the tabor. in which Mr. Harrison indulges
and which draws on him a rebuke from his critics the
severity of which one can also well understand. It is a
last fling at the *laus perennis,* which once seemed so beau-

tiful to monastic hearts, and which, looked at ideally, to those who can enter into Mr. Hutton's lofty view of adoration, means all that he describes. But practically it was a very poor, narrow, mechanical thing ; and base even when it represented, as it did to multitudes, the loftiest form of a soul's activity in such a sad, suffering world as this. I, for one, can understand, though I could not utter, the anathema which follows it as it vanishes from sight. And it bears closely on the matter in hand. It is no dead, mediæval idea. It tinctures strongly the popular religious notions of heaven. The favourite hymns of the evangelical school are set in the same key. There is an easy, self-satisfied, self-indulgent temper in the popular way of thinking and praying, and above all of singing, about heaven, which, sternly as the singers would denounce the cloister, is really caught from the monastic choir. There is a very favourite verse which runs thus :

> "There, on a green and flowery mount,
>   Our weary souls shall sit,
>   And with transporting joys recount
>   The labours of our feet." [1]

It is a fair sample of the staple of much pious forecasting of the occupations and enjoyments of heaven. I cannot but welcome very heartily any such shock as Mr. Harrison administers to this restful and self-centred vision of immortality. Should he find himself at last en-

---

[1] Mr. Martin's picture of "The Plains of Heaven" exactly presents it, and it is a picture greatly admired in the circles of which we speak,

dowed with the inheritance which he refuses, and be thrown in the way of these souls mooning on the mount' it is evident that he would feel tempted to give them a vigorous shake, and to set them with some stinging words about some good work for God and for their world. And as many of us want the shaking now badly enough, I can thank him for it, although it is administered by an over-rough and contemptuous hand.

I feel some hearty sympathy, too, with much which he says about the unity of the man. The passage to which I refer commences with the words "The philosophy which treats man as man simply affirms that man loves, thinks, acts, not that the ganglia, the senses, or any organ of man, loves, thinks, and acts."

So far as Mr. Harrison's language and line of thought are a protest against the vague, bloodless, bodiless notion of the life of the future, which has more affinity with Hades than with Heaven, I heartily thank him for it. Man is an embodied spirit, and wherever his lot is cast he will need and will have the means of a spirit's manifestation to and action on its surrounding world. But this is precisely what is substantiated by the resurrection. The priceless value of the truth of the resurrection lies in the close interlacing and interlocking of the two worlds which it reveals. It is the life which is lived here, the life of the embodied spirit, which is carried through the veil and lived there. The wonderful powers of the gospel of "Jesus and the resurrection" lay in the homely human interest which it lent to the life of the immortals. The risen Lord took up life just where he left it. The things which he had taught His disciples to care about here, were the things which those who had passed on were caring about there, the reign of truth, righteousness and love. I hold to the truth of the resurrection, not only because it appears to be firmly established on the most valid testimony, but because it alone seems to explain man's constitution as a spirit embodied in flesh which he is sorely tempted to curse as a clog. It furnishes to man the key to the mystery of the flesh on the one hand, while on the other it justifies his aspiration and realizes his hope.

Belief in the risen and reigning Christ was at the heart of that wonderful uprising and outburst of human energy which marked the age of the Advent. The contrast is most striking between the sad and even despairing tone which breathes through the noblest heathen literature which utters perhaps its deepest wail in the cry of Epictetus, "Show me a Stoic—by Heaven, I long to see a Stoic!" and the sense of victorious power, of buoyant, exulting hope, which breathes through the word and shines from the life of the infant Church: "As dying, and behold we live; as sorrowful, yet always rejoicing; as poor, yet making many rich ; as having nothing, and yet possessing all things." The Gospel which brought life and immortality to light won its way just as dawn wins its way, when "jocund day stands tiptoe on the misty mountain-tops," and flashes his rays over a sleeping world. Everywhere the radiance penetrates; it shines into every nook of shade ; and all living creatures stir, awake, and come forth to bask in its beams. Just thus the flood of kindling light streamed forth from the resurrection, and spread like the dawn in the morning sky; it touched all forms of things in a dark, sad world with its splendour and called man forth from the tomb in which his higher life seemed to be buried, to a new career of fruitful, sunlit activity; even as the Saviour prophesied, "The hour is coming, and now is, when the dead shall hear the voice of the Son of God, and they that hear shall live."

The exceeding readiness and joyfulness with which the truth was welcomed, and the measure in which Christendom—and that means all that is most powerful and progressive in human society—has been moulded by it, are the most notable facts of history. Be it truth, be it fiction, be it dream, one thing is clear: it was a baptism of new life to the world which was touched by it, and it has been near the heart of all the great movements of human society from that day until now. I do not even exclude "the Revolution," whose current is under us still. Space is precious, or it would not be difficult to show how deeply the Revolution was indebted to the ideas which this gospel brought into the world. I entirely agree with Lord Blachford that revelation is the ground on which faith securely rests. But the history of the quickening and the growth of Christian society is a factor of enormous moment in the estimation of the arguments for the truth of immortality. We are assured that the idea had the dullest and even basest origin. Man has a shadow, it suggested the idea of a second self to him! he has memories of departed friends, he gave them a body and made them ghosts! Very wonderful, surely, that mere figments should be the strongest and most productive things in the whole sphere of human activity, and should have stirred the spirit and led the march of the strongest, noblest, and most cultivated peoples; until now, in this nineteenth century, we think that we have discovered, as Miss Martineau tersely puts it, that " the theological belief of almost everybody in the civilized world is baseless." Let who will believe it, I cannot.

It may be urged that the idea has strong fascination, that man naturally longs for immortality, and gladly catches at any figment which seems to respond to his yearning and to justify his hope. But this belief is among the clearest, broadest, and strongest features of his experience and history. It must flow out of something very deeply imbedded in his constitution. If the force that is behind all the phenomena of life is responsible for all that is, it must be responsible for this also. Somehow man, the masterpiece of the Creation, has got himself wedded to the belief that all things here have relations to issues which lie in a world that is behind the shadow of death. This belief has been at the root of his highest endeavour and of his keenest pain; it is the secret of his chronic unrest. Now Nature, through all her orders, appears to have made all creatures contented with the conditions of their life. The brute seems fully satisfied with the resources of his world. He shows no sign of being tormented by dreams; his life withers under no blight of re-

gret. All things rest, and are glad and beautiful in their
spheres. Violate the order of their nature, rob them of
their fit surroundings, and they grow restless, sad, and
poor. A plant shut out from light and moisture will
twist itself into the most fantastic shapes, and strain itself to ghastly tenuity; nay, it will work its delicate tissues through stone walls or hard rock, to find what its
nature had made needful to its life. Having found it,
it rests and is glad in its beauty once more. Living things,
perverted by human intelligent effort, revert swiftly the
moment that the pressure is removed. This marked
tendency to reversion seems to be set in Nature as a sign
that all things are at rest in their natural conditions, content with their life and its sphere. Only in ways of
which they are wholly unconscious, and which rob them
of no contentment with their present, do they prepare the
way for the higher developments of life.

What then, means this restless longing in man for that
which lies beyond the range of his visible world? Has
Nature wantonly and cruelly made man, her masterpiece
alone of all the creatures, restless and sad? Of all beings
in the Creation must he alone be made wretched by an
unattainable longing, by futile dreams of a visionary
world? This were an utter breach of the method of Nature in all her operations. It is impossible to believe
that the harmony that runs through all her spheres fails
and falls into discord in man. The very order of Nature
presses us to the conviction that this insatiable longing
which somehow she generates and sustains in man, and

which is unquestionably the largest feature of his life, is not visionary and futile, but profoundly significant; pointing with firm finger to the reality of that sphere of being to which she has taught him to lift his thoughts and aspirations, and in which he will find, unless the prophetic order of the Creation has lied to him, the harmonious completeness of his life.

And there seems to be no fair escape from the conclusion by giving up the order, and writing Babel on the world and its life. Whatever it is, it is not confusion. Out of its disorder, order palpably grows; out of its confusion arises a grand and stately progress. Progress is a sacred word with Mr. Harrison. In the progress of humanity he finds his longed-for immortality. But, if I may repeat in other terms a remark which I offered some time ago, while progress is the human law, law, the world, the sphere of the progress, is tending slowly but inevitably to dissolution. Is there discord again in this highest region? Mr. Harrison writes of an immortal humanity. How immortal, if the glorious progress is striving to accomplish itself in a world of wreck? Or is the progress that of a race born with sore but joyful travail from the highest level of the material creation into a higher region of being, whence it can watch with calmness the dissolution of all the perishable worlds?

The belief in immortality is so dear to man because he grasps through it the complement of his else unshaped and imperfect life. It seems to be equally the complement of this otherwise hopelessly jangled and disordered

10

world. It is asked triumphantly, "Why, of all the hosts of creatures, does man alone lay claim to this great inheritance?" Because in man alone we see the experiences, the strain, the anguish, that demand it, as the sole key to what he does and endures. There is to me something horrible in the thought of such a life as ours, in which for all of us, in some form or other, the cross must be the most sacred symbol, lived out in that bare, heartless, hopeless world of the material, to which Prof. Clifford so lightly limits it. And I cannot but think that there are strong signs in many quarters of an almost fierce revulsion from the ghastly drearihood of such a vision of life.

There seems to me to run through Mr. Harrison's utterances on these great subjects—I say it with honest diffidence of one whose large range of power I so fully recognize, but one must speak frankly if this Symposium is to be worth anything—an instinctive yearning toward Christian ideas, while that faith is denied which alone can vivify them, and make them a living power in our world. There is everywhere a shadowy image of a Christian substance; but it reminds one of that formless form, wherein "what seemed a . head, the likeness of a kingly crown had on." And it is characteristic of much of the finest thinking and writing of our times. The saviour Deronda, the prophet Mordecai, lack just that living heart of faith which would put blood into their pallid lineaments, and make them breathe and move among men. Again I say that we have largely ourselves to thank for this saddening feature of the higher life of our times—we who have narrowed God's great kingdom to the dimensions of our little theological sphere. I am no theologian, though intensely interested in the themes with which the theologians occupy themselves. Urania, with darkened brow, may, perhaps, rebuke my prating. But I seem to see quite clearly that the sad strain and anguish of our life, social, intellectual, and spiritual, is but the pain by which great stages of growth accomplish themselves. We have quite outgrown our venerable, and in its time large and noble, theological shell. We must wait, not fearful, far less hopeless, while by the help of those who are working with such admirable energy, courage, and fidelity, outside the visible Christian sphere, that spirit in man which searches and cannot but search " the deep things of God," creates for itself a new instrument of thought which will give to it the mastery of a wider, richer, and nobler world.

Dr. W. G. WARD.

MR. HARRISON considers that the Christian's conception of a future life is "so gross, so sensual, so indolent, so selfish," as to be unworthy of respectful consideration. He must necessarily be intending to speak of this conception in the shape of which we Christians entertain it; because otherwise his words of reprehension are unmeaning. But our belief as to the future life is intimately and indissolubly bound up with our belief as to the present; with our belief as to what is the true measure and standard of human action in this world. And I would urge that no part of our doctrine can be rightly apprehended, unless it be viewed in its connection with all the rest. This is a fact which (I think) infidels often drop out of sight, and for that reason fail of meeting Christianity on its really relevant and critical issues.

Of course, I consider Catholicity to be exclusively the one authoritative exhibition of revealed Christianity. I will set forth, therefore, the doctrine to which I would call attention, in that particular form in which Catholic teachers enounce it; though I am very far indeed from intending to deny that there are multitudes of non-Catholic Christians who hold it also. What, then, according to Catholics, is the true measure and standard of human action? This is in effect the very first question propounded in our English elementary Catechism: "Why did God make you?" The prescribed answer is, "To know him, serve him, and love him in this world, and to be happy with him forever in the next." And St. Ignatius's "Spiritual Exercises"—a work of the very highest authority among us—having laid down the very same "foundation," presently adds that "we should not wish on our part for health rather than for sickness, wealth rather than poverty, honour rather than ignominy; desiring and choosing those things alone which are more expedient to us for the end for which we were created." Now, what will be the course of a Christian's life in proportion as he is profoundly imbued with such a principle as this, and vigorously aims at putting it into practice? The number of believers, who apply themselves to this task with reasonable consistency, is no doubt comparatively small. But in proportion as any given person does so, he will in the first place be deeply penetrated with a sense of his moral weakness; and (were it for that reason alone) his life will more and more be a life of prayer. Then he will necessarily give his mind with great earnestness and frequency to the consideration what it is which at this or that period God desires at his hands. On the whole (not to dwell with unnecessary detail on this part of my subject), he will be ever opening his heart to Almighty God; turning to him for light and strength under emergencies, for comfort under affliction; pondering on his adorable attributes; animated toward him by intense love and tenderness. Nor need I add how singularly—how beyond words—this personal love of God is promoted and facilitated by the fact that a Divine Person has assumed human nature, and that God's human acts and words are so largely offered to the loving contemplation of redeemed souls.

In proportion, then, as a Christian is faithful to his creed, the thought of God becomes the chief joy of his life. "The thought of God," says F. Newman, "and nothing short of it, is the happiness of man; for though there is much besides to serve as the subject of knowledge, or motive for action, or instrument of excitement, yet the *affections* require a something more vast and more enduring than anything created. He alone is sufficient for the heart who made it. The contemplation of him, and nothing but it, is able fully to open and relieve the mind, to unlock, occupy, and fix our affections. We may indeed love things created with great intenseness; but such affection, when disjoined from the love of the Creator, is like a stream running in a narrow channel, impetuous, vehement, turbid. The heart runs out, as it were, only at one door; it is not an expanding of the whole man. Created natures cannot open to us, or elicit, the ten thousand mental senses which belong to us, and through which we really love. None but the presence of our Maker can enter us; for to none besides can the whole heart in all its thoughts and feelings be unlocked and subjected. It is this feeling of simple and absolute confidence and communion which soothes and satisfies those to whom it is vouchsafed. We know that even our nearest friends enter into us but partially, and hold intercourse with us only at times; whereas the consciousness of a perfect and enduring presence, and it alone, keeps the heart open. Withdraw the object on which it rests, and it will relapse again into its state of confinement and constraint; and in proportion as it is limited, either to certain seasons or to certain affections, the heart is straitened and distressed."

Now, Christians hold that God's faithful servants will enjoy hereafter unspeakable bliss, through the most intimate imaginable contact with him whom they have here so tenderly loved. They will see face to face him whose beauty is dimly and faintly adumbrated by the most exquisitely transporting beauty which can be found on earth ; him whose adorable perfection they have in this life imperfectly contemplated, and for the fuller apprehension of which they have so earnestly longed here below. I by no means intend to imply that the hope of this blessedness is the sole or even the chief inducement which leads saintly men to be diligent in serving God. Their immediate. reason for doing so is their keen sense of his claim on their allegiance ; and, again, the misery which they would experience, through their love of him, at being guilty of any failure in that allegiance. Still the prospect of that future bliss, which I have so imperfectly sketched, is doubtless found by them at times of invaluable service in stimulating them to greater effort, and in cheering them under trial and desolation.

Such is the view taken by Christians of life in heaven; and, surely, any candid infidel will at once admit that it is profoundly harmonious and consistent with their view of what should be man's life on earth. To say that their anticipation of the futuie, *as it exists in them*, is gross, sensual, indolent, and selfish, is so manifestly beyond the mark that I am sure Mr. Harrison will, on reflection, retract his affirmation. Apart, however, from this particular comment, my criticism of Mr. Harrison would be this : He was bound, I maintain, to consider the Christian theory of life *as a whole ;* and not to dissociate that part of it which concerns eternity from that part of it which concerns time.

And now as to the merits of this Christian theory. For

my own part, I am, of course, profoundly convinced that,
as on the one hand it is guaranteed by revelation, so on
the other hand it is that which alone harmonizes with
the dicta of reason and the facts of experience, so far as
it comes into contact with these.   Yet I admit that
various very plausible objections may be adduced against
its truth.   Objectors may allege very plausibly that by
the mass of men it cannot be carried into practice : that
it disparages most unduly the importance of things secu-
lar ; that it is fatal to what they account genuine
patriotism ; that it has always been, and will always be,
injurious to the progress of science ; above all, that it
puts men (as one may express it) on an entirely wrong
scent, and leads them to neglect many pursuits which, as
being sources of true enjoyment, would largely enhance
the pleasurableness of life.   All this, and much more may
be urged, I think, by antithesists with very great superficial plausibility ; and the Christian controversialist is
bound on occasion steadily to confront it.   But there is
one accusation which has been brought against this
Christian theory of life—and that the one mainly (as
would seem) felt by Mr. Harrison—which to me seems so
obviously destitute of foundation that I find difficulty in
understanding how any infidel can have persuaded himself of its truth : I mean the accusation that this theory
is a *selfish* one.   There is no need of here attempting a
philosophical discussion on the respective claims of what
are now called " egoism " and " altruism :" a discussion in
itself (no doubt) one of much interest and much im-

portance, and one, moreover, in which I should be quite prepared (were it necessary) to engage. Here, however, I will appeal, not to philosophy, but to history. In the records of the past we find a certain series of men, who stand out from the mass of their brethren, as having preëminently concentrated their energy on the love and service of God, and preëminently looked away from earthly hopes to the prospect of their future reward. I refer to the saints of the Church. And it is a plain matter of fact, which no one will attempt to deny, that these very men stand out no less conspicuously from the rest in their self-sacrificing and (as we ordinary men regard it) astounding labours in behalf of what they believe to be the highest interests of mankind.

Before I conclude, I must not omit a brief comment on one other point, because it is the only one on which I cannot concur with Lord Blachford's masterly paper. I cannot agree with him that the doctrine of human immortality fails of being supported by " conclusive reasoning." I do not, of course, mean that the dogma of the Beatific Vision is discoverable apart from revelation ; but I do account it a truth cognizable with certitude by reason, that the human soul is naturally immortal, and that retribution of one kind or another will be awarded us hereafter, according to what our conduct has been in this our state of probation. Here, however, I must explain myself. When theists make this statement, sometimes they are thought to allege that human immortality is sufficiently proved by *phenomena ;* and sometimes they are thought to allege that it is almost intuitively evident. For myself, however, I make neither of these allegations. I hold that the truth in question is conclusively established by help of certain premises; and that these premises themselves can previously be known with absolute certitude, on grounds of reason or experience.

They are such as these : 1. There exists that Personal Being, infinite in all perfections, whom we call God. 2. He has implanted in his rational creatures the sense of right and wrong ; the knowledge that a deliberate perpetration of certain acts intrinsically merits penal retribution. 3. Correlatively, he has conferred freedom on the human will ; or in other words, has made acts of the human will exceptions to that law of uniform sequence which otherwise prevails throughout the phenomenal world.[1] 4. By the habit of prayer to God we can obtain augmented strength for moral action, in a degree which would have been quite incredible antecedently to experience. 5. Various portions of our divinely given nature clearly point to an eternal destiny. 6. The conscious self or ego is entirely heterogeneous to the material world : entirely heterogeneous, therefore, to that palpable body of ours which is dissolved at the period of death.

I do not think any one will account it extravagant to hold that the doctrine of human immortality is legiti-

---

[1] I shall not, of course, be understood to deny the existence and frequency of miracles.

mately deducible from a combination of these and similar
truths. The anti-theist will of course deny that they
are truths. Mr. Greg, who has himself " arrived at no
conviction" on the subject of immortality, yet says that
considerations of the same kind as those which I have
enumerated " must be decisive " in favour of immortality
" to all to whose spirits communion with their Father is
the most absolute of verities."[1]   Nor have I any reason
to think that even Mr. Huxley and Mr. Harrison, if they
could concede my premises, would demur to my conclusion.

MR. FREDERIC HARRISON.

I HAVE now, not so much to close a symposium, or
general discussion, as to reply to the convergent fire of
nine separate papers.   Neither time, nor space, nor the indulgence of the reader, would enable me to do justice to the
weight of this array of criticism, which reaches me in frag-
ments while I am otherwise occupied abroad.   I will ask
those critics whom I have not been able to notice to believe
that I have duly considered the powerful appeals they
have addressed to me.   And I will ask those who are
interested in this question to refer to the original papers
in which my views were stated.   And I will only add,
by way of reply, the following remarks, which were, for

------

[1] *See* his letter in the London *Spectator* of August 25th, 1877.

the most part, written and printed, while I had nothing
before me but the first three papers in this discussion.
They contain what I have to say on the theological, the
metaphysical, and the materialist aspect of this question.
For the rest, I could only repeat what I have already
said in the two original essays.

Whether the preceding discussion has given much new
strength to the doctrine of man's immaterial soul and
future existence I will not pretend to decide. But I cannot feel that it has shaken the reality of man's posthumous
influence, my chief and immediate theme. It seemed to
me that the time had come, when, seeing how vague and
hesitating were the prevalent beliefs on this subject, it
was most important to remember that, from a purely
earthly point of view, man had a spiritual nature, and
could look forward after death to something that marked
him off from the beasts that perish. I cannot see that
what I urged has been in substance displaced; though
much criticism (and some of it of a verbal kind) has been
directed at the language which I used of others. My
object was to try if this life could not be made richer;
not to destroy the dreams of another. But has the old
doctrine of a future life been in any way strengthened?
Mr. Hutton, it is true, has a "personal wish" for a perpetuity of volition. Lord Blachford "believes because he
is told." And Prof. Huxley knows of no evidence that
"such a soul and a future life exist;" and he seems not to
believe in them at all.

Philosophical discussion must languish a little, if, when

we ask for the philosophical grounds for a certain belief, we find one philosopher believing because he has a " personal wish " for it, and another " believing because he is told." Mr. Hutton says that, as far as he knows, " the thoughts, affections, and volitions, are not likely to perish with his body." Prof. Huxley seems to think it just as likely that they should. Arguments are called for to enable us to decide between these two authorities. And the only argument we have hitherto got is Mr. Hutton's " personal wish," and Lord Blachford's *ita scriptum est.* I confess myself unable to continue an argument which runs into believing " because I am told." It is for this reason that the *lazzarone* at Naples believed in the blood of St. Januarius.

My original propositions may be stated thus':

1. Philosophy as a whole (I do not say specially biological science) has established a functional relation to exist between every fact of thinking, willing, or feeling, on the one side, and some molecular change in the body on the other side.

2. This relation is simply one of correspondence between moral and physical facts, not one of assimilation. The moral fact does not become a physical fact, is not adequately explained by it, and must be mainly studied as a moral fact, by methods applicable to morals—not as a physical fact, by methods applicable to physics.

3. The moral facts of human life, the laws of man's mental, moral, and affective nature, must consequently be studied, as they have always been studied, by direct

observation of these facts ; yet the correspondence, specially discovered by biological science, between man's mind and his body, must always be kept in view. They are an indispensible, inseparable, but subordinate part of moral philosophy.

4. We do not diminish the supreme place of the spiritual facts in life and in philosophy by admitting these spiritual facts to have a relation with molecular and organic facts in the human organism—provided that we never forget how small and dependent is the part which the study of the molecular and organic phenomena must play in moral and social science.

5. Those whose minds have been trained in the modern philosophy of law cannot understand what is meant by sensation, thought, and energy, existing without any basis of molecular change ; and to talk to them of sensation, thought and energy, continuing in the absence of any molecules whatever, is precisely such a contradiction in terms as to suppose that civilization will continue in the absence of any men whatever.

6. Yet man is so constituted as a social being that the energies which he puts out in life mould the minds, characters, and habits, of his fellow-men ; so that each man's life is, *in effect*, indefinitely prolonged in human society. This is a phenomenon quite peculiar to man and to human society, and of course depends on there being men in active association with each other. Physics and biology can teach us nothing about it ; and physicists and biologists may very easily forget its importance. It can

be learned only by long and refined observations in moral
and mental philosophy as a whole, and in the history of
civilization as a whole.

7. Lastly, as a corollary, it may be useful to retain the
words soul and future life for their associations; provided
we make it clear that we mean by soul the combined faculties of the *living* organism, and by future life the subjective effect of each man's objective life on the actual
lives of his fellow-men.

I. Now, I find in Mr. Hutton's paper hardly any attempt to disprove the first six of these propositions. He
is employed for the most part in asserting that his hypothesis of a future state is a more agreeable one than mine,
and in earnest complaints that I should call his view of a
future state a selfish or personal hope. As to the first, I
will only remark that it is scarcely a question whether
his notion of immortality is beautiful or not, but whether
it is true. If there is no rational ground for expecting
such immortality to be a solid fact, it is to little purpose
to show us what a sublime idea it would be if there were
anything in it. As to the second, I will only say that I
do not call his notion of a future existence a selfish or
personal hope. In the last paragraph of my second
paper I speak with respect of the opinion of those who
look forward to a future of moral development instead of
to an idle eternity of psalm-singing. My language as to
the selfishness of the vulgar ideas of salvation was directed to those who insist that, unless they are to *feel* a
continuance of pleasure, they do not care for any continu-

ance of their influence at all. The vulgar are apt to say
that what they desire is the sense of personal satisfaction,
and, if they cannot have this, they care for nothing else.
This, I maintain, is a selfish and debasing idea. It is the
common notion of the popular religion, and its tendency
to concentrate the mind on a merely personal salvation
does exert an evil effect on practical conduct. I once
heard a Scotch preacher, dilating on the narrowness of the
gate, etc., exclaim, "O dear brethren, who would care to
be saved *in a crowd ?*"

I do not say this of the life of grander activity in
which Mr. Hutton believes, and which Lord Blachford so
eloquently describes. This is no doubt a fine ideal, and
I will not say other than an elevating hope. But on what
does it rest ? Why this ideal rather than any other ?
Each of us may imagine, as I said at the outset, his own
Elysian fields, or his own mystic rose. But is this philosophy ? Is it even religion ? Besides, there is this
other objection to it: It is not Christianity, but Neo-
Christianity. It is a fantasia with variations on the
orthodox creed. There is not a word of the kind in the
Bible. Lord Blachford says he believes in it "because he
is told." But it so happens that he is not told this, at
any rate in the creeds and formularies of orthodox faith.
If this view of future life is to rest entirely on revelation,
it is a very singular thing that the Bible is silent on the
matter. Whatever kind of future ecstacy may be suggested in some texts, certain it is that such a glorified energy as Lord Blachford paints in glowing colours is no-

where described in the Bible. There is a constant practice nowadays, when the popular religion is criticised,
that earnest defenders of it come forward exclaiming :
" Oh ! that is only the vulgar notion of our religion. My
idea of the doctrine is so and so," something which the
speaker has invented without countenance from the offi-
cial authority. For my part, I hold Christianity to be
what is taught in average churches and chapels to the
millions of professing Christians. And I say it is a very
serious fact when philosophical defenders of religion begin
by repudiating that which is taught in average pulpits.

Perhaps a little more attention to my actual words
might have rendered unnecessary the complaints in all
these papers as to my language about the hopes which
men cherish for the future. In the first place I freely
admit that the hopes of a grander energy in heaven are
not open to the charge of vulgar selfishness. I said that
they are unintelligible, not that they are unworthy. They
are unintelligible to those who are continually alive to the
fact I have placed as my first proposition—*that every
moral phenomenon is in functional relation with some
physical phenomenon*. To those who deny or ignore this
truth, there is, doubtless, no incoherence in all the ideals
so eloquently described in the papers of Mr. Hutton and
Lord Blachford. But, once get this conception as the
substratum of your entire mental and moral philosophy,
and it is as incoherent to talk to us of your immaterial
development as it would be to talk of obtaining redness
without any red thing.

11

I will try to explain more fully why this idea of a
glorified activity implies a contradiction in terms to those
who are imbued with the sense of correspondence between physical and moral facts.   When we conceive any
process of thinking, we call up before us a complex train
of conditions : objective facts outside of us, or the re-
vived impression of such facts ; the molecular effect of
these facts upon certain parts of our organism, the association of these with similar facts recalled by memory, an
elaborate mechanism to correlate these impressions, an
unknown to be made known, and a difficulty to be overcome.   All systematic thought implies relations with the
external world present or recalled, and it also implies
some shortcoming in our powers of perfecting those relations.   When we meditate, it is on a basis of facts which
we are observing, or have observed and are now recalling,
and with a view to get at some result which baffles our
direct observation and hinders some practical purpose.

The same holds good of our moral energy.   Ecstasy
and mere adoration exclude energy of action.   Moral development implies difficulties to be overcome, qualities
balanced against one another under opposing conditions,
this or that appetite tempted, this or that instinct tested
by proof.   Moral development does not grow like a fun-
gus ; it is a continual struggle in surrounding conditions
of a specific kind, and an active putting forth of a variety of practical faculties in the midst of real obstacles.

So, too, of the affections : they equally imply conditions.   Sympathy does not spurt up like a fountain in

the air ; it implies beings in need of help, evils to be alle-
viated, a fellowship of giving and taking, the sense of
protecting and being protected, a pity for suffering, an
admiration of power, goodness and truth. All of these
imply an external world to act in, human beings and objects, and human life under human conditions.

Now, all these conditions are eliminated from the orthodox ideal of a future state. There are to be no physical
impressions, no material difficulties, no evil, no toil, no
struggle, no human beings, and no human objects. The
only condition is a complete absence of all conditions, or
all conditions of which we have any experience. And we
say, we cannot imagine what you mean by your intensi-
fied sympathy, your broader thought, your infinitely
varied activity, when you begin by postulating the absence of all that makes sympathy, thought, and activity
possible, all that makes life really noble.

A mystical and inane ecstacy is an appropriate ideal
for this paradise of negation, and this is the orthodox
view ; but it is not a high view. A glorified existence of
greater activity and development may be a high view,
but it is a contradiction in terms ; exactly, I say, as if you
were to talk of a higher civilization without any human
beings. But this is simply a metaphysical after-thought
to escape from a moral dilemma. Mr. Hutton is surely
mistaken in saying that Positivists have forgotten that
Christians ever had any meaning in their hopes of a
" beatific vision." He must know that Dante and Thomas
à Kempis form the religious books of Positivists, and they

are, with some other manuals of Catholic theology, among the small number of volumes which Comte recommended for constant use. We can see in the celestial " visions " of a mystical and unscientific age, much that was beautiful in its time, though not the highest product even of theology. But in our day, these visions of paradise have lost what moral value they had, while the progress of philosophy has made them incompatible with our modern canons of thought.

Mr. Hutton supposes me to object to any continuance of sensation as an evil in itself. My objection was not that consciousness should be .prolonged in immortality, but that nothing else but consciousness should be prolonged. All real human life, energy, thought, and active affection, are to be made impossible in your celestial paradise, but you insist on retaining consciousness. To retain the power of feeling, while all means and objects are taken away from thinking, all power of acting, all opportunity of cultivating the faculties of sympathy are stifled; this seems to me something else than a good. It would seem to me that simply to be conscious, and yet to lie thoughtless, inactive, irresponsive, with every faculty of a man paralyzed within you, as if by that villainous drug which produces torpor while it intensifies sensation—such a consciousness as this must be a very place of torment.

I think some contradictions, which Mr. Hutton supposes he detects in my paper, are not very hard to reconcile. I admitted that death is an evil, it seems; but I spoke of our posthumous activity as a higher kind of influence. We might imagine, of course, a Utopia, with neither suffering, waste, nor loss; and compared with such a world, the world, as we know it, is full of evils, of which death is obviously one. But relatively, in such a world as alone we know, death becomes simply a law of organized Nature, from which we draw some of our guiding motives of conduct. In precisely the same way the necessity of toil is an evil in itself; but, with man and his life as we know them, we draw from it some of our highest moral energies. The grandest qualities of human nature, such as we know it at least, would become forever impossible if Labour and Death were not the law of life.

Mr. Hutton again takes but a pessimist view of life when he insists how much of our activity is evil, and how questionable is the future of the race. I am no pessimist, and I believe in a providential control over all human actions by the great Power of Humanity, which indeed brings good out of evil, and assures, at least for some thousands of centuries, a certain progress toward the higher state. Pessimism, as to the essential dignity of man and the steady development of his race, is one of the surest marks of the enervating influence of this dream of a celestial glory. If I called it as wild a desire as to go roving through space in a comet, it is because I can attach no meaning to a *human* life to be prolonged without a human frame and a human world; and it seems to me as rational to talk of becoming an angel as to talk of becoming an ellipse.

By " duties " of the world beyond the grave, I meant the duties which are imposed on us in life, by the certainty that our action must continue to have an indefinite effect. The phrase may be inelegant, but I do not think the meaning is obscure.

II. I cannot agree with Lord Blachford that I have fallen into any confusion between a substance and an attribute. I am quite aware that the word " soul " has been hitherto used for some centuries as an entity. And I proposed to retain the term for an attribute. It is a very common process in the history of thought. Electricity, life, heat, were once supposed to be substances. We now very usefully retain these words for a set of observed conditions or qualities.

I agree with Mr. Spencer that the unity of the social organism is quite as complete as that of the individual organism. I do not confuse the two kinds of unity ; but I say that man is in no important sense a unit that society is not also a unit.

With regard to the " percipient " and the "perceptible" I cannot follow Lord Blachford. He speaks a tongue that I do not understand. I have no means of dividing the universe into " percipients " and "perceptibles." I know no reason why a "percipient" should not be a "perceptible," none why I should not be " perceptible," and none why beings about me should not be " perceptible." I think we are all perfectly " perceptible "—indeed, some of us are more " perceptible " than "percipient"—though I cannot say that Lord Blachford is always "perceptible " to me. And how

does my being "perceptible" or not being "perceptible,"
prove that I have an immortal soul? Is a dog "perceptible?" is he "percipient?" Has he not some of the
qualities of a "percipient?" and if so, has he an immortal
soul? Is an ant, a tree, a bacterium, "percipient?" and
has any of these an immortal soul? for I find Lord Blachford declaring there is an "ineradicable difference between
the motions of a material and the sensations of a living
being," as if the animal world were "percipient," and the
inorganic "perceptible." But surely in the sensations of
a living being the animal world must be included. Where
does the vegetable world come in?

I used the word "organism" advisedly, when I said
that will, thought, and affection, are functions of a living
organism. I decline exactly to localize the organ of any
function of mind or will. When I am asked, What are
we? I reply, We are men. When I am asked, Are we our
bodies? I say, No, nor are we our minds. Have we no
sense of personality, of unity? I am asked. I say, Certainly; it is an acquired result of our nervous organization, liable to be interrupted by derangements of that
nervous organization. What is it that makes us think
and feel? The facts of our human nature; I cannot get
behind this, and I need no further explanation. We are
men, and can do what men can do. I say the tangible
collection of organs known as a "man" (not the consensus
or the condition, but the *man*), thinks, wills, and feels,
just as much as that visible organism lives and grows.
We do not say that this or that ganglion in particular

lives and grows; we say the *man* grows. It is as easy to
me to imagine that we shall grow fifteen feet high, when
we have no body, as that we shall grow in knowledge,
goodness, activity, etc., etc., etc., when we have no organs.
And the absence of all molecular attributes would be, I
should think, particularly awkward in that life of comet-
ary motion in the interstellar spaces with which Lord
Blachford threatens us. But, as the poet says:

> " Trasumanar significar per verba
> Non si porria "—

" *If,*" says he, " practical duties are necessary for the perfection of life," we can take a little interstellar exercise.
Why, practical duties are the sum and substance of life ;
and life which does not centre in practical duties is not
life, but a trance.

Lord Blachford, who is somewhat punctilious in terms,
asks me what I consider myself to understand " by the
incorporation of a consensus of faculties with a glorious
future." Well, it so happens that I did not use that phrase.
I have never spoken of an immortal soul anywhere, nor
do I use the word soul of any but the living man. I said
a man might look forward to incorporation with the
future of his race, explaining that to mean his " posthumous activity." And I think at any rate the phrase is
quite as reasonable as to say that I look forward, as Mr.
Hutton does, to a " union with God." What does Mr.
Hutton or Lord Blachford understand himself to mean by
that ?

Surely Lord Blachford's epigram about the fiddle and the tune is hardly fortunate. Indeed, that exactly expresses what I find faulty in the view of himself and the theologians. He thinks the tune will go on playing when the fiddle is broken up and burned. I say nothing of the kind. I do not say the man will continue to exist after death. I simply say that his influence will; that other men will do and think what he taught them to do or to think. Just so, a general would be said to win a battle which he planned and directed, even if he had been killed in an early part of it. What is there of fiddle and tune about this? I certainly think that when Mozart and Beethoven have left us great pieces of music, it signifies little to art if the actual fiddle, or even the actual composer continue to exist or not. I never said the tune would exist. I said that men would remember it and repeat it. I must thank Lord Blachford for a happy illustration of my own meaning. But it is *he* who expects the tune to exist without the fiddle. *I* say you can't have a tune without a fiddle, nor a fiddle without wood.

III. I have reserved the criticism of Prof. Huxley, because it lies apart from the principal discussion, and turns mainly on some incidental remarks of mine on " biological reasoning about spiritual things."

I note three points at the outset. Prof. Huxley does not himself pretend to any evidence for a theological soul and future life. Again, he does not dispute the account I give of the functional relation of physical and moral facts. He seems surprised that I should understand it,

not being a biologist; but he is kind enough to say that
my statement may pass. Lastly, he does not deny the
reality of man's posthumous activity. Now, these three
are the main purposes of my argument; and in these I
have Prof. Huxley with me. He is no more of a theologian than I am. Indeed, he is only scandalized that I
should see any good in priests at all. He might have said
more plainly that, when the man is dead, there is an end
of the matter. But this clearly is his opinion, and he in-
timates as much in his paper. Only he would say no
more about it, bury the carcass, and end the tale, leaving
all thoughts about the future to those whose faith is more
robust and whose hopes are richer; by which I understand him to mean persons weak enough to listen to the
priests.

Now, this does not satisfy me. I call it materialism,
for it exaggerates the importance of the physical facts
and ignores that of the spiritual facts; and the object of
my paper was simply this that as the physical facts
are daily growing quite irresistible, it is of urgent importance to place the spiritual facts on a sound scientific
basis at once. Prof. Huxley implies that his business is
with the physical facts, and the spiritual facts must take
care of themselves. I cannot agree with him. That is
precisely the difference between us. The spiritual facts
of man's nature are the business of all who undertake to
denounce priestcraft, and especially of those who preach
" Lay Sermons."

Prof. Huxley complains that I should join in the view-

halloo against biological science. Now, I never have supposed that biological science was in the position of the
hunted fox. I thought it was the hunter, booted and
spurred and riding over us all, with Prof. Huxley leaping
the most terrific gates and cracking his whip with intense
gusto. As to biological science, it is the last thing that I
should try to run down; and I must protest, with all sin-
cerity, that I wrote without a thought of Prof. Huxley
at all. He insists on knowing, in the most peremptory
way of whom I was thinking, as if I were thinking of
him. Of whom else could I be thinking, forsooth, when
I spoke of biology? Well! I did not bite my thumb at
him, but I bit my thumb.

Seriously, I was not writing at Prof. Huxley, or I
should have named him. I have a very great admiration
for his work in biology; I have learned much from him;
I have followed his courses of lectures years and years
ago, and have carefully studied his books. If, in questions
which belong to sociology, morals, and to general philosophy, he seems to me hardly an authority, why need we
dispute? Dog should not bite dog; and he and I have
many a wolf that we both would keep from the fold.

But, if I did not mean Prof. Huxley, whom did I mean?
Now, my paper, I think clearly enough, alluded to two
very different kinds of materialism. There is systematic
materialism, and there is the vague materialism. The
eminent example of the first is the unlucky remark of
Cabanis that the brain secretes thought, as the liver secretes bile; and there is much of the same sort in many

foreign theories—in the tone of Moleschott, Büchner, and the like. The most distinct examples of it in this country are found among phrenologists, spiritualists, some mental pathologists, and a few communist visionaries. The far wider, vaguer, and more dangerous school of materialism is found in a multitude of quarters—in all those who insist exclusively on the physical side of moral phenomena—all, in short, who, to use Prof. Huxley's phrase, are employed in "building up a physical theory of moral phenomena." Those who confuse moral and physical phenomena are indeed few. Those who exaggerate the physical side of phenomena are many.

Now, though I did not allude to Prof. Huxley in what I wrote, his criticism convinces me that he is sometimes at least found among these last. His paper is an excellent illustration of the very error which I condemned. The issue between us is this: We both agree that every mental and moral fact is in functional relation with some molecular fact. So far we are entirely on the same side, as against all forms of theological and metaphysical doctrine which conceive the possibility of human feeling without a human body. But, then, says Prof. Huxley, if I can trace the molecular facts which are the antecedents of the mental and moral facts, I have *explained* these mental and moral facts. That I deny; just as much as I should deny that a chemical analysis of the body could ever lead to an explanation of the physical organism. Then, says the professor, when I have traced out the molecular facts, I have built up a *physical theory of moral phenomena.* That again I deny. I say there is no such thing, or no rational thing, that can be called a physical theory of moral phenomena, any more than there is a moral theory of physical phenomena. What sort of a thing would be a physical theory of history— history *explained* by the influence of climate or the like? The issue between us centres in this: I say that the physical side of moral phenomena bears about the same part in the moral sciences that the facts about climate bear in the sum of human civilization. And that to look to the physical facts as an explanation of the moral, or even as an independent branch of the study of moral facts, is perfectly idle; just as it would be if a mere physical geographer pretended to give us, out of his geography, a climatic philosophy of history. Yet Prof. Huxley has not been deterred from the astounding paradox of proposing to us a *physiological theory of religion.* He tells us how " the religious feelings may be brought within the range of physiological inquiry." And he proposes as a problem—" *What diseased viscus may have been responsible for the 'priest in absolution?'* " I will drop all epithets; but I must say that I call that materialism, and materialism not very nice of its kind. One might as reasonably propose as a problem—What barometrical readings are responsible for the British Constitution? and suggest a congress of meteorologists to do the work of Hallam, Stubbs, and Freeman. No doubt there is *some* connection between the House of Commons and the English climate, and so there is no doubt *some* connection between religious theories and physical organs. But to talk of " bringing religion within the range of physiological inquiry " is simply to stare through the wrong end of the telescope, and to turn philosophy and science upside down. Ah! Prof. Huxley, this is a bad day's work for scientific progress—

ἣ κεν γηθήσαι Πρίαμος, Πριάμοιό τε παῖδες.

Pope Pius[1] and his people will be glad when they read that fatal sentence of yours. When I complained of the "attempt to dispose of the deepest moral truths of human nature on a bare physical or physiological basis," I could not have expected to read such an illustration of my meaning by Prof. Huxley.

Perhaps he will permit me to inform him (since that is the style which he affects) that there once was—and, indeed, we may say still is—an institution called the Catholic Church; that it has had a long and strange history, and subtile influences of all kinds; and I venture to think that Prof. Huxley may learn more about the *priest in absolution* by a few weeks' study of the Catholic system than by inspecting the diseased *viscera* of the whole human race. When Prof. Huxley's historical and religious studies " have advanced so far as to enable him to explain " the history of Catholicism, I think he will admit that "priestcraft" cannot well be made a chapter in a physiological manual. It may be cheap pulpit thunder, but this idea of his of inspecting a " diseased viscus " is

---

[1] This was written previous to the death of Pope Pius IX.

precisely what I meant by "biological reasoning about spiritual things." And I stand by it, that it is just as false in science as it is deleterious in morals. It is an attempt (I will not say arrogant, I am inclined to use another epithet) to explain, by physical observations, what can only be explained by the most subtile moral, sociological, and historical observations. It is to think you can find the golden eggs by cutting up the goose, instead of watching the goose to see where she lays the eggs.

I am quite aware that Prof. Huxley has elsewhere formulated his belief that biology is the science which " includes man and all his ways and works." If history, law, politics, morals, and political economy, are merely branches of biology, we shall want new dictionaries indeed ; and biology will embrace about four-fifths of human knowledge. But this is not a question of language ; for we here have Prof. Huxley actually bringing religion within the range of *physiological* inquiry, and settling its problems by references to " diseased viscus." But the differences between us are a long story ; and since Prof. Huxley has sought me out, and in somewhat monitorial tone has proposed to set me right, I will take an early occasion to try and set forth what I find paradoxical in his notions of the relations of biology and philosophy.

I note a few special points between us, and I have done. Prof. Huxley is so well satisfied with his idea of a "physical theory of moral phenomena," that he constantly attributes that sense to my words, though I carefully guarded my language from such a construction. Thus

he quotes from me a passage beginning, " Man is one,
however compound," but he breaks off the quotation just
as I go on to speak of the direct analysis of mental and
moral faculties by mental and moral science, not by physiological science. I say : " philosophy and science " have
accomplished explanations; I do not say biology ; and
the biological part of the explanation is a small and subordinate part of the whole. I do not say that the correspondence between physical and moral phenomena is an
explanation of the human organism. Prof. Huxley says
that, and I call it materialism. Nor do I say that " spiritual sensibility is a *bodily* function." I say, it is a moral
function ; and I complain that Prof. Huxley ignores the
distinction between moral and physical functions of the
human organism.

As to the distinction between anatomy and physiology,
if he will look at my words again, he will see that I use
these terms with perfect accuracy. Six lines below the
passage he quotes, I speak of the human mechanism being
only explained by a " complete anatomy *and biology*,"
showing that anatomy is merely one of the instruments
of biology.

He might be surprised to hear that he does not himself
give an accurate definition of physiology. But so it is.
He says, " Physiology is the science which treats of the
functions of the living organism." Not so, for the finest
spiritual sensibility is, as Prof. Huxley admits, a function
of living organism ; and physiology is not the science
which treats of spiritual sensibilities. They belong to

moral science. There are mental, moral, affective functions of the living organism ; and they are not within the province of physiology. Physiology is the science which treats of the *bodily* functions of the living organism ; as Prof. Huxley says in his admirable "Elementary Lessons," it deals with the facts " concerning the action of the *body.*" I complain of the pseudo-science which drops that distinction for a minute. He says, "The explanation of a physiological function is the demonstration of the connection of that function with the molecular state of the organ which exerts the function." That I dispute. It is only a small part of the explanation. The explanation substantially is the demonstration of the laws and all the conditions of the function. The explanation of the circulation of the blood is the demonstration of all its laws, modes, and conditions ; and the molecular antecedents of it are but a small part of the explanation. The principal part relates to the molar (and not the molecular) action of the heart and other organs. " The function of motion is explained," he says, " when the movements of the living body are found to have certain molecular changes for their invariable antecedents." Nothing of the kind. The function of bodily motion is explained when the laws, modes, and conditions, of that motion are demonstrated ; and molecular antecedents are but a part of these conditions. The main part of the explanation, again, deals with molar, not molecular, states of certain organs. "The function of sensation is explained," says Prof. Huxley, " when the molecular changes, which are the invariable

12

antecedents of sensations, are discovered." Not a bit of
it. The function of sensation is only explained when the
laws and conditions of sensation are demonstrated. And
the main part of this demonstration will come from direct
observation of the sensitive organism organically, and by
no molecular discovery whatever. All this is precisely
the materialism which I condemn ; the fancying that one
science can do the work of another, and that any molecular discovery can dispense with direct study of organisms
in their organic, social, mental, and moral aspects. Will
Prof. Huxley say that the function of this Symposium is
explained, when we have chemically analyzed the solids
and liquids which are now effecting molecular change in
our respective digestive apparatus ? If so, let us ask the
butler if he cannot produce us a less heady and more mel-
low vintage. What irritated *viscus* is responsible for the
materialist in philosophy? We shall all philosophize
aright, if our friend Tyndall can hit for us the exact
chemical formula for our drinks.

It does not surprise me, so much as it might, to find
Prof. Huxley slipping into really inaccurate definitions in
physiology, when I remember that hallucination of his
about questions of science all becoming questions of molecular physics. The molecular facts are valuable enough;
but we are getting molecular-mad, if we forget that molecular facts have only a special part in physiology, and
hardly any part at all in sociology, history, morals, and
politics ; though I quite agree that there is no single fact
in social, moral, or mental philosophy, that has not its

correspondence in some molecular fact, if we only could know it. All human things undoubtedly depend on, and are certainly connected with, the general laws of the solar system. And to say that questions of human organisms, much less of human society, tend to become questions of molecular physics, is exactly the kind of confusion it would be, if I said that questions of history tend to become questions of astronomy, and that the more refined calculations of planetary movements in the future will explain to us the causes of English Rebellion and the French Revolution.

There is an odd instance of this confusion of thought at the close of Prof. Huxley's paper, which still more oddly Lord Blachford, who is so strict in his logic, cites with approval. "Has a stone a future life," says Prof. Huxley, "because the wavelets it may cause in the sea persist through space and time?" Well! has a stone a *life* at all? because if it has no present life, I cannot see why it should have a future life. How is any reasoning about the inorganic world to help us here in reasoning about the organic world? Prof. Huxley and Lord Blachford might as well ask if a stone is capable of civilization because I said that man was. I think that man is wholly different from a stone; and from a fiddle; and even from a dog; and that to say that a man cannot exert any influence on other men after his death, because a dog cannot, or because a fiddle or because a stone cannot, may be to reproduce with rather needless affectation the verbal quibbles and pitfalls which Socrates and the sophists prepared for each other in some wordy symposium of old.

Lastly, Prof. Huxley seems to think that he has disposed of me altogether, so soon as he can point to a sympathy between theologians and myself. I trust there are great affinity and great sympathy between us; and pray let him not think that I am in the least ashamed of that common ground. Positivism has quite as much sympathy with the genuine theologian as it has with the scientific specialist. The former may be working on a wrong intellectual basis, and often it may be by most perverted methods; but, in the best types, he has a high social aim and a great moral cause to maintain among men. The latter is usually right in his intellectual basis as far as it goes; but it does not go very far, and in the great moral cause of the spiritual destinies of men he is often content with utter indifference and simple nihilism. Mere raving at priestcraft, and beadles, and outward investments, is indeed a poor solution of the mighty problems of the human soul and of social organization. And the instinct of the mass of mankind will long reject a biology which has nothing for these but a sneer. It will not do for Prof. Huxley to say that he is only a poor biologist and careth for none of these things. His biology, however, "includes man and all his ways and works." Besides, he is a leader in Israel; he has preached an entire volume of "Lay Sermons;" and he has waged many a war with theologians and philosophers on religious and philosophic problems. What, if I may ask him, are his own religion and his own philosophy? He says that he knows no scientific men who "neglect all philosophical and religious synthesis." In that he is fortunate in his circle of acquaintances. But since he is so earnest in asking me questions, let me ask him to tell the world what is his own synthesis of philosophy, what is his own idea of religion? He can laugh at the worship of priests and positivists: whom, or what, does he worship? If he dislikes the word soul, does he think that man has anything that can be called a spiritual nature? If he derides my idea of a future life, does he think that there is anything which can be said of a man, when his carcass is laid beneath the sod, beyond a simple final *vale?*

P.S.—And now space fails me to reply to the appeals of so many critics. I cannot enter with Mr. Roden Noel on that great question of the materialization of the spirits of the dead; I know not whether we shall be "made one with the great Elohim, or angels of Nature, or if we shall grovel in dead material bodily life." I know nothing of this high matter: I do not comprehend this language. Nor can I add anything to what I have said on that sense of personality which Lord Selborne and Canon Barry so eloquently press on me. To me that sense of personality is a thing of somewhat slow growth, resulting from our entire nervous organization and our composite mental constitution. It seems to me that we can often trace it building up and trace it again decaying away. We feel ourselves to be *men*, because we have human

bodies and human minds. Is that not enough ? Has the
baby of an hour this sense of personality ? Are you sure
that a dog or an elephant has not got it ? Then has the
baby no soul ; has the dog a soul ? Do you know more
of your neighbour, apart from inference, than you know
of the dog ? Again, I cannot enter upon Mr. Greg's
beautiful reflections, save to point out how largely he
supports me. He shows, I think with masterly logic,
how difficult it is to fit this new notion of a glorified
activity on to the old orthodoxy of beatific ecstacy.
Canon Barry reminds us how this orthodoxy involved the
resurrection of the body, and the same difficulty has
driven Mr. Roden Noel to suggest that the material world
itself may be the *débris* of the just made perfect. But
Dr. Ward, as might be expected, falls back on the beatific
ecstacy as conceived by the mystics of the thirteenth
century. No word here about moral activity and the
social converse, as in the Elysian fields, imagined by
philosophers of less orthodox severity.

One word more. If my language has given any believer pain, I regret it sincerely. It may have been somewhat obscure, since it has been so widely arraigned, and
I think misconceived. My position is this : The idea of
a glorified energy in an ampler life is an idea utterly
incompatible with exact thought, one which evaporates
in contradictions, in phrases which when pressed have no
meaning. The idea of beatific ecstacy is the old and
orthodox idea ; it does not involve so many contradictions
as the former idea, but then it does not satisfy our moral

judgment. I say plainly that the hope of such an infinite ecstacy is an inane and unworthy crown of a human life. And when Dr. Ward assures me that it is merely the prolongation of the saintly life, then I say the saintly life is an inane and unworthy life. The words I used about the " selfish " views of futurity, I applied only to those who say they care for nothing but personal enjoyment, and to those whose only aim is "to save their own souls." Mr. Baldwin Brown has nobly condemned this creed in words far stronger than mine. And here let us close with the reflection that the language of controversy must always be held to apply not to the character of our opponents, but to the logical consequences of their doctrines, if uncorrected and if forced to their extreme.

THE INFLUENCE UPON MORALITY

OF A

DECLINE IN RELIGIOUS BELIEF.

INFLUENCE UPON MORALITY

OF A

DECLINE IN RELIGIOUS BELIEF.

SIR JAMES STEPHEN.

M ANY persons regard everything which tends to discredit theology with disapprobation, because they think that all such speculations must endanger morality as well. Others assert that morality has a basis of its own in human nature, and that, even if all theological belief were exploded, morality would remain unaffected.

My own view is, that each party is to a considerable extent right, but that the true practical inference is often neglected.

Understanding by the theology of an age or country the theory of the universe generally accepted then and there, and by its morality the rules of life then and there commonly regarded as binding, it seems to me extravagant to say that the one does not influence the other. The difference between living in a country where the established theory is that existence is an evil, and annihilation the highest good, and living in a country where the established theory is that the earth is the Lord's and the fullness thereof, the round world and they that dwell therein, has surely a good deal to do with the other differences which distinguish Englishmen from Buddhists.

Even if it be said that such differences are merely a way of expressing the result of a difference of temperament and constitution otherwise caused, this does not diminish the effect of a belief in the truth of the theory. Kali, Bhowanee, and other malevolent deities worshipped in India, are probably phantoms engendered by fear working on a rank fancy; but this does not make the belief in their real existence less influential in those who hold it. A man who cuts off the end of his tongue to propitiate Kali would let it alone if he ceased to believe in her existence, though the temper of mind which created her might still remain, and show itself in other ways.

The belief that the course of the world is ordered by a good God, that right and wrong are in the nature of a divine law, that this world is a place of trial, and part only of a wider existence—in a word, the belief in God and a future state—may be accounted for in various ways. Now that in this country (to go no farther) the vast majority of people believe these doctrines to be true, in fact, just as they believe it to be true, in fact, that ships and carriages can be driven by steam, and that their conduct is in innumerable instances as distinctly influenced

by the one belief as by the other, appear to me to be pro
positions too plain to be proved.

On the other hand, it seems at least equally evident
that morality has a basis of its own quite independent of
all theology whatever. It is difficult to imagine any
doctrine about theology which has not prevailed at some
time or place; but no one ever heard of men living together without some rules of life—that is, without some
sort of morality. Given human action and human passion, and a vast number of people all acting and feeling,
moral rules of conduct of some sort are a necessary consequence. The destruction of religion would, I think, involve a moral revolution; but it would no more destroy
morality than a political revolution destroys law. It
would substitute one set of moral rules and sentiments for
another, just as the establishment of Christianity and
Mohammedanism did when they superseded various forms
of paganism.

It would be scarcely worth while to write down these
commonplaces, if it were not for the sake of the practical
inference. It is that theology and morality ought to
stand to each other in precisely the same relation as facts
and legislation.

No one would propose to support by artificial means
a law passed under a mistake, for fear it should have to
be altered. To say that the truth of a theological doctrine
must not be questioned, lest the discovery of its falsehood
should produce a bad moral effect, is in principle precisely
the same thing. It is at least as unlikely that false

theology should produce good morals as that legislation based on a mistaken view of facts should work well in practice.

I will give two illustrations of this—any number might be given: Suicide is commonly regarded as wrong; and this moral doctrine is defended on theological grounds, which are summed up in the old saying that the soldier must not leave his post till he is relieved. I will not inquire whether any other argument can be produced forbidding suicide to a person labouring under a disease which converts his whole life into one long scene of excruciating agony, and which must kill him in the course of a few useless months, during which he is a source of misery, and perhaps danger, to his nearest and dearest friends. I confine myself to saying that, if it could be shown that there is no reason to suppose that God has in fact forbidden such an act, its morality might be discussed and decided upon on different grounds from those, on which it must be considered and decided upon on the opposite hypothesis.

Take again, the law of marriage. Suppose a man's wife is hopelessly insane—ought he be allowed to marry again ? Ought divorce to be permitted in any case ? These questions will be discussed in a very different spirit, though it is possible that they might be answered in the same way by persons who do and by persons who do not believe in sacraments, and that marriage is a sacrament.

Now, let us suppose for the sake of argument that it could be shown that, if all theological considerations were set aside, it would be desirable that a person dying of cancer should be permitted to commit suicide, and that a man whose wife was incurably mad should be allowed to marry again ; and that, on the other hand, if theological considerations were taken into account, the opposite was desirable. Upon these suppositions the question whether the theological beliefs which make the difference are beneficial or not will depend on the question whether they are true or not. Applied generally, this shows that the support which an existing creed gives to an existing system of morals is irrelevant to its truth, and that the question whether a given system of morals is good or bad cannot be fully determined until after the determination of the question whether the theology on which it rests is true or false. The morality is good if it is founded on a true estimate of the consequences of human actions. But if it is founded on a false theology, it is founded on a false estimate of the consequences of human actions; and, so far as that is the case, it cannot be good ; and the circumstance that it is supported by the theology to which it refers is an argument against, and not in favour of, that theology.

LORD SELBORNE.

I BEGIN by observing that (putting special cases aside, and looking at the question in a general way) morality has not flourished, among either civilized or uncivilized men, when religious belief has been generally lost, or utterly debased. Not to dwell upon the case of savage races, the modern Hindoos and Chinese have long been civilized, but are certainly not moral ; nor can anything worse be conceived than the morality of the Greeks and Romans, at the height of their civilization. The morality of the Romans, in the old republican times when they knew nothing of Greek philosophy, was praised by Polybius, who connected it, directly and emphatically, with the influence among them of religious belief. After their intellectual cultivation had taken its tone from the irreligious or agnostic materialism of Epicurus (hardly distinguishable, I think, from that sort of philosophy which some persons think destined to supplant religious belief in the present day), their morality became what is described in the first chapter of the Epistle to the Romans and in the Satires of Juvenal ; nor does it seem to have been worse than that of the other civilized races on the shores of the Mediterranean, over whom, at the same time, religion had equally lost its influence.

On the other hand, it seems to me certain, as an historical fact, that the place which the principles of love and benevolence, humility and self-abnegation, have assumed in the morality of Christian nations (with a wide-spreading influence which has been advancing till the present time with the growth of civilization) is specifically due to Christianity. To Christianity are specially due—1. Our respect for human life, which condemns suicide, infanticide, political assassination, and I might almost say homicide generally, in a way previously unknown, and still unknown where Christianity does not prevail; 2. recognition of such moral and spiritual relations between man and man as are inconsistent with the degradation of women, and with the practice of slavery; 3. Our reverence for the bond of marriage; and, 4. Our abhorrence of some particular forms of vice. I do not mean to deny that traces of a state of opinion, more or less similar upon some of these points, are discoverable in what we know of the manners of some non-Christian nations; but it is historically true to say that the prevalence of each of these principles, as manifested among ourselves, is specifically due to Christianity. Of Christianity I speak in a sense inclusive of all that it derives from the antecedent Jewish system; of which it claims to be the true continuation and development.

If freedom of inquiry is not to be stopped, after the rejection of religious belief, it must gradually extend itself to the whole circle of morality, most, if not all, of which is as little capable of demonstrative proof through the evidence of the senses as any of the doctrines of religion. Those who reject religion will not voluntarily submit to moral restraints founded upon the religion which they reject, unless they can be placed upon some other intellectual basis, sufficiently cogent to themselves to resist the attractions of appetite or self-interest. That large part of mankind who are always too much under the government of their inclinations and passions will be quicker in drawing moral corollaries from irreligious principles than the philosophers by whom those principles are propounded;

13

and the advanced posts of morality, in which the influence
of religion culminates, and of which the necessity may
not be so evident on natural or social grounds, are not
likely to be very strenuously defended by those philosophers themselves.

If the religious foundations and sanctions of morality
are given up, what is to be substituted for them?

First: will the modern notion of a duty to act so as may
conduce to the greatest happiness of the greatest number
of men be sufficient? I think, certainly not. The idea
of duty is not, to my mind, practical or intelligible without
religious conceptions; and this particular conception of
duty depends entirely upon a test extrinsic, and not personal, to the individual—a test, too, which it is difficult
(not to say impossible) for each individual to verify for
himself; though it may be verified, to their own satisfaction, by philosophical students of casuistry or political
economy. Those motives are of necessity strongest which
directly concern the man himself: and a moral principle
which attempts to counteract influences operating directly
and immediately upon the will by others which are
speculative and remote, without any higher sanctions
realized by and reacting upon the individual, must necessarily be weak.

But, secondly: will this idea be sufficient, if so modified
as to present to the man the pursuit of his own happiness
in this world as the rule of life, but teach him to discover
it by observing and doing those things which most conduce to the happiness of men in general? In this form it

is older and more plausible ; but the difficulties of making it practical are really very much the same. This doctrine, as Aristotle observes, depends upon a general induction : it deals only with general truths and general conclusions, to which there are many apparent and (if there were no law of moral retribution and adjustment behind) many real exceptions. The foundations of a man's moral character and habits must be laid in his youth : when (as Aristotle also says) he is inexperienced, naturally inclined to follow his passions, and not predisposed to accept the disquisitions of philosophers as proof that his own happiness will not be promoted by seeking it in his own way. The temperament most likely to act consciously on such a rule of life is not the most generous ; it is rather that which is cold and calculating, and which values the reputation more than the reality of virtue. Upon such men, at the best, its influence is to establish a low standard of virtue : perhaps only to check and impose limits on their tendency to vice. Over others it can have little or no power, except when operating in combination with, and subordination to, higher principles.

Not only did the ethical systems of the ancients which were based upon this principle fail to make men moral, but we see its impotence constantly exemplified among those whom we call " men of the world "—a class of persons who are by no means indifferent to their own happiness, or to the good opinion of the world, but by whom the influence of religious belief is not practically felt ; exemplified, too, on points of morality of which the reasonableness seems most manifest. There are no virtues, I suppose, which can more readily be shown to be conducive to happiness, whether particular or general, than that which the Greeks called ἐγκρατεία, and that of benevolence. What can be more contrary, to both at once of these, than the irregular indulgence of sensual appetite at the cost of the permanent degradation, and almost certain misery, of human beings who are its instruments and victims, and of innumerable physical as well as moral evils to individuals, families, and mankind at large? Yet how very common is this sort of immorality, even among cultivated men, living on good terms with society! How little is it reproved, how seldom restrained, except by the authority, or through the influence, direct or indirect, of religion! All readers of Horace remember the *sententia dia Catonis*, and I doubt whether non-religious opinion among ourselves is much stricter on this subject, though it may be less freely expressed. If it is otherwise as to some of the more abnormal forms of ἀκρασία, I have already said that is specifically due to Christianity. The cultivated Greeks and Romans spoke and wrote lightly and familiarly of vices of which we do not speak at all: they regarded them, indeed, as effeminate, but not as infamous, and certainly did not visit them with grave social penalties. So tainted was their moral atmosphere, that even such really religious men among them as Socrates and Plato (to whom, however, a religion teaching morals with definiteness and authority was unknown) surprise us by their want of sensitiveness on these points, as manifested in some passages of the Socratic Dialogues.

· I will next inquire whether a sufficient rule of morality is to be found, when religion is set aside, in any law of our nature : first, regarding the constitution of our nature apart from, and, secondly, taking into account, the existence in it, of a moral instinct or sense.

If any one calls the application of right reason to human conduct generally a law of our nature, from which such a rule is to be derived, without taking into account the moral sense—this, as it seems to me, would be only a different and more indefinite mode of expressing substantially the same theories, which have been already dealt with.

But it may, perhaps, be suggested that laws of our nature, from which such a rule may be derived, are to be found in the final causes and purposes of the several organs and powers which exist in that nature ; and that the use of any of those organs or powers in a manner aberrant from their proper causes and purposes is a breach of natural morality. I do not pause to inquire whether the idea of " cause " and " purpose," which is involved in such a view, can be verified apart from religion. But such a rule would, at best, be far from co-extensive with the whole field of morality ; some most necessary parts of a moral code (such, e. g., as the regulation of the relations between the sexes) being incapable of being deduced, with any approach to certainity, from the mere constitution of our nature. As to some of our faculties, the determination, with sufficient accuracy, to furnish a rule of life, of their final causes and purposes, might involve difficult philosophical inquiries. As to others, though there might be no such difficulty, it is to be remembered that we have a complex nature, in which the forces which operate, either mechanically or in a way resembling the mechanical, · upon the will, are constantly in practical antagonism to the regulative faculty. The faculties of which the final causes are most obvious exist, not apart from, but in combination with, other elements of our nature which (either generally or often) result in tendencies to their use without any direct view to the fulfilment of their proper purposes. The gratification of some of those tendencies (such, e. g., as eating and drinking for the mere pleasure of taste, and not for nourishment) can hardly be condemned as immoral, on natural grounds, unless carried so far as to overpower reason, or impair strength or health. When it is carried to that excess (as in the case of intemperance), it is still true that the origin of the vice has been in the natural constitution of men's bodies, by which a sensible gratification has been found in its indulgence : which (as it seems to me) goes far to prove that this conception of a physical law cannot be relied upon, even in the cases to which it is most directly applicable, as a practical basis of morality —a view which is confirmed by the actual prevalence among men of that class of vices, even when, to all natural safeguards, is superadded the external influence of religion.

When we proceed to take into account the moral instinct or sense, we come upon the border-ground, if not into the proper territory, of Religion. To a man who believes in a moral government of the universe, in the distinctness of the *Ego*, the real man, from his bodily organization, and in the doctrines of moral responsibility and moral adjustment in a future state, nothing can be more real, nothing more intelligible, than this moral instinct or sense, with its suggestions of right and wrong, of duty, guilt and sin, and its judicial conscience. But, if all these postulates are denied, what is then to be thought of this moral instinct or sense? Why is it, on that hypothesis, less a mere accident of the nervous system, or of some other part of the bodily organization, than the religious instinct, which is already supposed to be set aside, as resting upon no demonstrable ground? As a phenomenon, and in some sense a fact, it exists, just as the religious instinct does (if they be not really the same); but those principles of thought which explain away the one, as having no proper objective cause, and as indicative of no objective truth, may as easily explain away the other also. The one is not more susceptible of sensible and experimental demonstration than the other. If man were merely a higher order of the organization of matter, homogeneous with, and produced by spontaneous development from inorganic substances, plants, and inferior animals, and under no responsibility to any moral intelligence greater than his own, what reality would there be in the conception of a moral law of obligation, inapplicable to all other known forms of matter, and applicable only to man,

These questions are practical. Experience, on the large scale, shows that men who disregard the religious, cannot generally be trusted to pay regard to the moral, sense. A moral sense, not believed in, can never supply a practical foundation for morality. On the other hand, a moral sense, believed in, is (in reality) itself religion—possibly inarticulate, but religion still. Such a belief cannot exist, without accepting the evidence of the moral sense as equally trustworthy concerning those things of which it informs us, as the evidence of the bodily senses is concerning those things of which they inform us. It is, of course, only from the impressions made upon our own minds that we can know anything about any of the subjects, either of physical, or of intellectual, or of moral sensation: their intrinsic nature, abstracted from those impressions, is to us, in each case alike, an inaccessible mystery. But belief in the sense is belief in the truth of the information which the sense gives to us; that is, that this information, if rightly apprehended, is trustworthy, as far as it goes; that there are objective realities corresponding with it. The moral sense, believed in, is not merely a possible, but I suppose it to be the only possible, human foundation of morality. An intelligent belief in the moral sense naturally takes the man beyond himself, to a higher source of his moral conceptions, which it really presupposes; and any truths correlative to it, which are either ascertainable by the processes of reason, or capable of being otherwise made known, will naturally, when they become known, be recognized, in their proper relation to it, and cannot be rejected without doing it violence. Any such correlative knowledge of the higher truths (to the existence of which the moral sense testifies, though it does not fully reveal them) must enlighten, inform, and strengthen it. It is the office of such knowledge to answer authoritatively those questions, as to the real nature, the proper work, the true happiness, the true place in the universe of man, which philosophy has always been asking and has never, by itself, been able to solve. It harmonizes, accounts for, and enforces by authoritative sanctions, the concurrent testimonies of the moral sense, the religious instinct, Nature interpreted by reason, and reason enlightened by experience. On the other hand, the want, and still more the rejection of such knowledge (supposing it to be attainable and true) must, in a corresponding degree, obscure, perplex, or discredit, the moral sense.

I am well aware that some who seem to reject all dogmatic theology and even the principles of natural religion, do nevertheless live up to a high moral standard; just as there are too many others, professing (not always insincerely) to believe in religion, who do the reverse. The moral sense never has been, and never will be, extinguished among mankind; and in all ages and countries, of which we have any real historical knowledge, there have been conspicuous examples of men who have made it their rule of life. Doubtless there have been many more who did so, of whom we know nothing; nor is it unreasonable to believe that there may be many such even among very degraded races. But these facts do not invalidate general conclu-

sions as to the general moral tendency of a decline of
religious belief. Those examples of exceptional goodness
have not been sufficient to prevent or to arrest a progressive deterioration of general morality when the light of
religion has been absent or obscured ; and the best ancient
schemes of philosophy, which were founded upon the
moral sense, failed to compete practically with that of
materialism, which did all that was possible to destroy it.
" Live while we may "—" let us eat and drink, for to-
morrow we die "—are natural corollaries from the doctrine
of Epicurus ; whatever more refined conceptions that
philosophers or any of his followers may have propounded.
Such will ever be the effect, in the world generally, of a
popular disbelief in the doctrines of immortality and retribution ; not because the hope of rewards or the fear of
punishments is the foundation of religious morality (which
to fulfil the requirements either of religion or of the
moral sense, must ascend much higher), but because our
nature is so constituted that the destiny of the individual,
for good or evil, for happiness or the reverse, is insepar-
ably bound up with the moral law of his being ; and
because those aids and defences which result from the
recognition of this truth are necessary for the ascendency
of the higher over the lower elements of our nature, and
for the education of man to virtue. A boy, whose main-
springs of right action are conscience and love, will not
endeavour to fulfil the objects for which he is sent to
school more selfishly, or from less worthy motives, when
he is informed of their relation to his future life, than if

he were left in ignorance of it; but the knowledge of that relation, by making him understand the importance of the future as compared with the present, and the meaning and reasonableness of his present duties, may enable him better to fulfil them.

All that has been said assumes, of course, that there is such a thing as religious truth: nor is it possible to deny that, if this could really be disproved, the morality founded upon it would fail. But it cannot be without importance, whenever the proper evidences of the truth of religion are considered, to take into account, as one of them, its relation to morality: the certainty that, if it were displaced, the system of morality now received among men would, to a great extent, fall with it; and the extreme intellectual difficulty of maintaining, in that event, the supremacy of the moral sense, or placing the morality of the future upon a new basis, likely to acquire general authority among mankind. If it should be suggested that a sufficient moral code, for practical purposes, might be maintained by increasing the stringency of human laws in proportion to the failure of religious sanctions, I should reply that the power of human laws depends upon morality, and not morality upon human laws; and that any legislation, greatly in advance of the moral sentiment of the community, would certainly not be effectual, and could not long be maintained.

It has been no part of my purpose to enter into an examination of any questions as to particular doctrines of religion. I have throughout used the word "religion" in a sense exclusive of all systems, usurping that name, which take no cognizance of morality, or which are repugnant, in their practical precepts, to the general moral sense of mankind; and I have not dissembled my belief that Christianity (regarded in its general aspect, with reference to the points of agreement rather than those of difference among Christians) does fulfil the conditions necessary for moral efficacy. Error, inconsistency, incompleteness, or admixture of foreign elements, in particular modes of apprehending or representing it, must, no doubt, as far as they prevail, and in proportion to their importance, detract from the authority, or deteriorate the quality, of its influence. So also must the mere fact of disagreement. But, notwithstanding all these drawbacks, Christianity is the great moral power of the world. It has often been supposed to be declining, but has, as often, renewed its strength; nor has any other power been found to take its place, where it has seemed to lose ground. As to other forms of religion it may, without difficulty, be admitted that such elements as they have in common with Christianity may be expected (except so far as they are neutralized or counteracted by other contrary elements) to tend, in their measure, toward the same standard of morality. It is proper (as I suppose) to Christianity, rightly understood, to assert the identity of its own essential principles with those of natural religion, while teaching that the moral government of the world has been so conducted as not to leave mankind dependent upon natural religion only; and it refers to a common origin with itself all the elements of religious belief, consistent with its own doctrines, which have been, at any time or place, accepted among the nations of the world. These propositions, and also that of the presence of the religious principle in any ·practical belief of the moral sense, appear to be in accordance with what is said by St. Paul in the nineteenth and twentieth verses of the first, and the fourteenth and fifteenth verses of the second chapter of the Epistle to the Romans.

REV. DR. MARTINEAU.

IN order to estimate aright the moral influence of declining religious belief, the relation between morals and religion must be accurately conceived. They may be regarded as independent, or as identical, or, again, either may be taken to be the foundation of the other. The following positions will serve as a sufficient ground for the opinion which I shall offer :

A sense of duty is inherent in the constitution of our nature, and cannot be escaped till we can escape from ourselves. It does not wait on any ontological conditions, and incur the risk of non-existence should no assurance be gained with regard to a being and a life beyond us. Even though we came out of nothing, and returned to nothing, we should be subject to the claim of righteousness so long as we are what we are. Morals have their own base, and are second to nothing.

Apart from this intrinsic consciousness of ethical distinctions, no ontological discoveries would avail to set up a law of duty, and give us the characteristics of moral beings. A Supreme Power might dictate an external rule, and break us in to obedience by hopes and fears of unlimited extent. But by this sway of preponderant interests we are not carried beyond prudence; and in the absence of a law within, responding to the demands from without, we do not reach the confines of moral obligation; and, in case of failure, we incur the sense only of error, not of sin. Theology cannot supply a base for morals that have lost their own.

Does it follow that, because morals are indigenous, they are therefore self-sufficing? By no means. Though religion is not their foundation, it is assuredly their crown —related to them as Plato says dialectic is to the sciences, ὥσπερ θριγκὸς τοῖς μαθήμασιν[1]—the *coping* that consummates them. Be the genesis of the conscience what it may, we learn from it at last that there is a better and a worse in the springs of action which contend for us, and that, while it is open to us as a possibility, it is closed against us as a right, to follow the lower when the higher calls. The *authority* which stamps the one as a temptation, and other as a peremptory claim, is not, we are well aware, of our own making; for it masters us with compunction, and defies all repeal. Nor is it the mere expression of public self-interest; for it extends beyond the range of social action, and covers the whole voluntary field. Speaking

---

[1] *Rep.*, vii., 534 E.

with a voice before which our whole personality bows, and which equally gives law to other men, it issues from a source transcending human life, and infusing into it a moral order from a more comprehensive sphere. It postulates a superior will in communion with ours, and administering this world as a school of character.

To this result our moral experience naturally runs up, and stops short of it only where its ·course is artificially arrested. Till it is reached, the ethical demands upon us seem to address us in tones too portentous for their immediate significance; remorse clings to us with a tenacity, aspiration returns upon us with a power, which reason cannot adequately justify. But in the presence of an objective moral law pervading the universe, administered by a Mind wherein it perfectly lives, and continued for man beyond his present term of years, the scale of the ethical passions, and the intensity of admiration and reverence for the good, fall into proportionate place, and escape the irony of being at once the ultimate nobleness and the supreme extravagance of our nature. Religion, on this side, is but the open blossom of the moral germs implanted within us—the explicit form, developed in thought, of faiths implicitly contained in the sense of responsibility and the foreboding of guilt. Its effect, therefore, is to suffuse with a divine light relations and duties which before were simply personal and social.

A similar transfiguration befalls the pleasures and pains attending voluntary conduct, and constituting its natural " sanctions." Treated as ultimate facts, they can never

acquire more than a prudential significance. Treated as
symbolical lineaments of a world under moral government,
they are invested with an expression of character, and
look into us with living eyes. Their appeal alights no
longer on self-regarding hope and fear, but on the springs
of sympathy and shame : they pass from sensitive to ethical phenomena. The new and ideal meaning thus given to
a large portion of actual human experience cannot pause
there ; it completes itself in the congenial anticipation of
a further and invisible store of awards consummating the
incipient justice of this world. The faith in a future life
—where it is more than a belief at second hand—has
its sheet-anchor in the moral affections. But for the felt
interval between what we are and what we ought to
be, for the indignation at wrong, for compassion toward
innocent suffering, and reverence for high excellence,
vaticinations of renewed existence would have no origin
and no support.

In assigning this method of growth to religion, I do not
mean to deny that it may have other lines of formation.
The Nature-worship which plays so great a part in ancient
civilization has a different history, and stands in much
less intimate relations with the moral life of its votaries.
We pay, I am disposed to think, too great a compliment
to the Greek mythology when we attribute the ethical
decay of later Athens and Corinth to the growing scepti-
cism about its gods. The public life was dead. The theatre of great passion and great action was closed. The
calls for sacrifice, the opportunities for national expansion
were gone, and the political school for the discipline of

character was no longer there. With the loss of a progressive history , the springs of heroic emulation suffered
atrophy, a sickly hue passed over literature, philosophy
and art : and the subsidence of human loves and cares
upon low Epicurean levels was inevitable, though the Olym-
pian deities had never been dethroned. In the *absence* of
any moral religion, no efficacious resistance could be set
up, with or without a pantheistic polytheism, against the
canker of social degeneracy.

In dealing with the present problem, however, we confine our attention to the Christian type of religion, which
has its hold upon our nature from the moral side. The
question is, what practical effect might be expected from
a decay of that religion.

Under that change morality would lose, not its base,
but its summit. The ground and principles of duty would
remain ; the means for deducing rules of action, estimating
the worth of conflicting impulses, and measuring the
grades of obligation, would in the main be unaffected ; so
that the moral code which would emerge from the labours
of a mere philosopher need not materially differ from that
recognized by a Christian. This is only an inverse method
of saying that the Christian ethics are true to human life
and the expression of right reason. I do not think, therefore, that the form and contents of a moral system would
be essentially modified by the decline of religious belief.
It may, no doubt, happen that particular problems of conduct, as in the cases of suicide and of marriage, have become the subjects of ecclesiastical legislation, and so have

14

passed into preoccupation of religious feeling, and, on the disappearance of that feeling, may be flung back into an indeterminate condition. But to the real solution of such problems it would be difficult to show that religion contributes any new elements, so as to turn into duty that which was not duty before. Its ministers and temporary interpreters can give an historical consecration to all sorts of ungrounded opinions, and these will in any case have to look out for an adequate base, whether or not the religious view of life is still upheld. But it is quite possible that a rule of life, once thoughtfully constituted, should be acknowledged in common over the whole range of social duty by persons simply ethical and by those who are also religious.

But though the decay of religion may leave the institutes of morality intact, it drains off their inward power. The devout faith of men expresses and measures the intensity of their moral nature, and it cannot be lost without a remission of enthusiasm, and under this low pressure, the successful reëntrance of importunate desires and clamorous passions which had been driven back. To believe in an ever-living and perfect Mind, supreme over the universe, is to invest moral distinctions with immensity and eternity, and lift them from the provincial stage of human society to the imperishable theatre of all being. When planted thus in the very substance of things, they justify and support the ideal estimates of the conscience; they deepen every guilty shame; they guarantee every righteous hope; and they help the will with a divine casting-vote in every balance of temptation. The sanctity thus given to the claims of duty, and the interest that gathers around the play of character, appear to me more important elements in the power of religion than its direct sanctions of hope and fear. Yet to these also it is hardly possible to deny great weight, not only as extending the range of personal interests, but as the answer of reality to the retributory verdicts of the moral sense. Cancel these beliefs, and morality will be left reasonable still, but paralyzed ; possible to temperaments comparatively passionless, but with no grasp on vehement and poetic natures ; and gravitating toward the simply prudential wherever it maintains its ground.

Historical experience appears to confirm this estimate. In no race (notwithstanding conspicuous individual exceptions) have the excesses of sensual passion been so kept in check as among the Jews. There is no more striking feature in their literature during the moral declension of Greek and Roman society (e. g„ in the Sibylline Oracles) than the horror which it expresses of the pervading dissoluteness of the pagan world. It certainly cannot be said that the problem was rendered easy by the coolness of the Jewish temperament. The phenomena of Christendom presents a more complicated tissue. But a just analysis yields, I believe, the same result, and attests the force of religious conviction as the only successful antagonist, on any large scale, of the animal impulses. True it is that, in the very presence of the Church, and even among its representatives, gross vices have at times prevailed. But these have been hollow times, in which, with large classes of persons, the outer shell of religion sheltered no sincere life, and the private habits betrayed the inward disintegration which policy or indifference concealed. To test the power of religion, we must limit ourselves to cases where that power is not effete. In the Puritan families of the seventeenth century, among the present Catholic peasantry of Ireland, throughout the Society of Friends, and in the Wesleyan classes, it can hardly be denied that the control of irregular desires has been attained with an exceptional ease and completeness.

One source of this distinctive power yet remains to be indicated. A simply conscientious man may surrender himself unreservedly to the sense of moral obligation, and be so possessed by it as to feel it more than reasonable, and own a certain sacredness in its appeal. Duty, honour, self-forgetfulness in other's good, may obtain the real command of such a one. But the persuasive force with which the right speaks to him is beyond all intellectual measure; it stirs him in depths he cannot reach; its heat is in excess of its light; it is something mystic which must have him, but of which he can render no account. Here, in truth, is religion pressing into life, only with form still indistinct, and its organism of thought not yet differentiated and articulate. Let it complete its development, and what change will ensue? Once rendered conscious of the Supreme Source of his moral perceptions, the responsible agent no longer obeys a pressure out of the dark, but rather a drawing toward higher light; for an impersonal

drift of Nature is substituted a profound personal veneration, and enthusiasm is turned from a blind nobleness into the clear allegiance of living affection. It is not without reason that this change has been treated as an emer-
gence into new life. Its vast influence is attested by the
whole literature of devotion, and especially by its most
popular element, the hymns of every age from the Psalter
to the " Christian Year."

Though in theory the contents of morality are not altered by acquiring divine obligation, the efficacy of religion
is more immediately felt in some parts of the character
than in others. The scene to which it introduces the mind
is one which throws it instantly into the attitude of looking up toward an Infinite Perfection, whose presence it
never quits, and thus supplies the true condition of humility, of aspiration, and of felt equality of moral trust for
all men before God. These moods of thought are specifically induced by the contract of higher excellence and a
most capacious rule of righteousness ; and they are but
poorly simulated by the mere sense of personal insignifi-
cance amid the immensity of Nature, and the awe of the
unknown, and the conscious partnership of us all in the
human liabilities. The moral characteristics of the Christian temper are nothing but the natural posture of a mind
standing face to face with the invisible reality of the highest ideals of its conscience and its love. If that presence
departs, they cannot survive.

MR. FREDERIC HARRISON.

AND all this, to me, describes the moral characteristics, not of the Christian, but of the religious temper. With what has been so finely said in the preceding discourse we ought, I think, most cordially to join. Only for the words "theology" and "Christian" we must put the wider and more ancient terms "religion" and "human;" and again, for the intrinsic consciousness and emotional intuitions, whereby these are said to prove themselves, we must substitute the reasonable proof of science, philosophy, and positive psychology.

We have had before us three distinctive views, as to the relations of religion and morality. Each of the three has pressed on us a very powerful thought. The reconciliation is obscure, yet I hold on to the hope that it may one day be found; that we shall have to surrender neither religion nor science, neither demonstration on the one hand, nor dogma, worship, and discipline, on the other; that we shall end by accepting a purely human base for our morality, and withal come to see our morality transfigured into a true religion.

It is the purport of the first of the arguments before us to establish: that morality has a basis of its own quite independent of all theology whatever; but that, since morality must be deeply affected by any theology, the morality will be undermined if based on a theology which is not true. We must all agree, I think, to that.

The second argument insists that, if the religious foundations and sanctions of morality be given up, human life runs the risk of sinking into depravity, since morality without religion is insufficient for general civilization. For my part, I entirely assent to that.

The third argument rejoins, that theology cannot supply a base for morals that have lost their own; but that morals, though they have their own base, and are second to nothing, are not adequate to direct human life until they be transfused into that sense of resignation, adoration, and communion with an overruling Providence, which is the true mark of religion. I assent entirely to that.

We, who follow the teaching óf Comte, humbly look forward to an ultimate solution of all such difficulties by the force of one common principle. That we acknowledge a religion, of which the creed shall be science; of which the faith, hope, charity, shall be real, not transcendental—earthly, not heavenly: a religion in a word, which is entirely human in its evidences, in its purposes, in its sanctions and appeals. Write the word "religion" where we find the word "theology;" write the word "human" where we find the word "Christian," or the words "theist," "Mussulman," or "Buddhist," and these discussions grow practical and easily reconciled; the aspirations and sanctions of religion burst open to us anew in greater intensity, without calling on us to surrender one claim of reality and humanity; the realm of faith and adoration becomes again conterminous with life, without disturbing—nay, while sanctifying—the invincible resolve of modern men to live *in* this world, *for* this world, *with* their fellow-men.

And this brings us to the source of all difficulties about the relations of morality and religion. We place our morality—we are compelled by the conditions of all our positive knowledge to place it—in a strictly human world. But it is the mark of every theology (the name of theology assumes it) to place our religion in a non-human world. And thus our human system of morals may possibly be distorted—it cannot be supported—by a non-human religion. But, on the other hand, it is dwarfed and atrophied for want of being duly expanded into a truly human religion. Our morality, with its human realities, our theology, with its non-human hypotheses, will not amalgamate. Their methods are in conflict. In their base, in their logic, in their aim, they are heterogeneous. They do not lie *in pari materiâ*. Give us a religion as truly human, as really scientific, as is our moral system, and all is harmony. Our morals based as they must be on our knowledge of life and of society, are then ordered and inspired by a religion which belongs, just as truly as our moral science does, to the world of science and of man. And then religion will be no longer that quicksand of possibility which two thousand years of debate have still left it to so many of us. It becomes, at last, the issue of our knowledge, the meaning of our science, the soul of our morality, the ideal of our imagination, the fulfilment of our aspirations, the law-giver, in short, of our whole lives. Can it ever be this while we still pursue religion into the bubble-world of the whence and the whither?

That morality is dependent on theology; that morality is independent of religion : each of these views presents insuperable difficulties, and brings us to an alternative from which we recoil. To assert that there is no morality but what is based on theology, is to assert what experience, history, and philosophy, flatly contradict —nay, that which revolts the conscience of all manly purpose within us. History teaches us that some of the best types of morality, in men and in races, have been found apart from anything that Christians can call theology at all. Morality has been advancing for centuries in modern Europe, while the theology, at least in authority, has been visibly declining. The morality of Confucius and of Sakya Mouni, of Socrates and Marcus Aurelius, of Vauvenargues, Turgot, Condorcet, Hume, was entirely independent of any theology. The moral system of Aristotle was framed without any view to theology, as completely as that of Comte or of our recent moralists. We have experience of men with the loftiest ideal of life and of strict fidelity to their ideal, who expressly repudiate theology, and of many more whom theology never touched. Lastly, there is a spirit within us which will not believe that to know and to do the right we must wait until the mysteries of existence and the universe are resolved—its origin, its government, and its future. To make right conduct a corollary of a theological creed, is not only contrary to

fact, but shocking to our self-respect. We know that
the just spirit can find the right path, even while the
judgment hangs bewildered amid the churches.

To hold, as would seem to require of us the second argument, that, though theology is necessary as a base for
morality, yet almost any theology will suffice—polytheist,
Mussulman, or deist—so long as some imaginary being is
postulated, this is, indeed, to reduce theology to a mini-
mum; since in this case, it does not seem to matter in
which God you may believe. To say that morality is
dependent on *one* particular theology, is to deny that
men are moral outside your peculiar orthodoxy; to say
that morality is dependent merely on *some* form of theology, is to say that it matters little to practical virtue
which of a hundred creeds you may profess. And when
we shrink from the arrogance of the first and the loose-
ness of the second position, we have no alternative but to
admit that our morality must have a human, and not a
super-human, base.

It does not follow that morality can suffice for life
without religion. Morality, if we mean by that the
science of duty, after all can supply us only with a knowledge of what we should do. Of itself it can neither touch
the imagination, nor satisfy the thirst of knowledge, nor
order the emotions. It tells us of human duty, but nothing of the world without us; it prescribes to us our duties,
but it does not kindle the feelings which are the impulse
to duty. Morality has nothing to tell us of a paramount
power outside of us, to struggle with which is confusion

and annihilation, to work with which is happiness and strength ; it has nothing to teach us of a communion with a great goodness, nor does it 'touch the chords of veneration, sympathy and love, within us. Morality does not profess to organize our knowledge and give symmetry to life. It does not deal with beauty, affection, adoration. If it order conduct, it does not correlate this conduct with the sum of our knowledge, or with the ideals of our imagination, or with the deepest of our emotions. To do all this is the part of religion, not of morality ; and inasmuch as the sphere of this function is both wider and higher, so does religion transcend morality. Morality has to do with conduct, religion with life. The first is the code of a part of human nature, the second gives its harmony to the whole of human nature. And morality can no more suffice for life than a just character would suffice for any one of us without intellect, imagination, or affection, and the power of fusing all these into the unity of a man.

The lesson, I think, is twofold. On the one hand, morality is independent of theology, is superior to it, is growing while theology is declining, is steadfast while theology is shifting, unites men while theology separates them, and does its work when theology disappears. There is something like a civilized morality, a standard of morality, a convergence about morality. There is no civilized theology, no standard of theology, no convergence about it. On the other hand, morality will never suffice for life ; and every attempt to base our existence with morality alone, or to crown our existence with morality alone, must certainly fail; for this is to fling away the most powerful motives of human nature. To reach these is the privilege of religion alone. And those who trust that the future can ever be built upon science and civilization, without religion, are attempting to build a pyramid of bricks without straw. The solution, we believe, is a non-theloogical religion.

There are some who amuse themselves by repeating that this is a contradiction in terms, that religion implies theology. Yet no one refuses the name of religion to the systems of Confucius and Buddha, though neither has a trace of theology. But disputes about a name are idle. If they could debar us from the name of religion, no one could disinherit us of the thing. We mean by religion a scheme which shall explain to us the relations of the faculties of the human soul within, of man to his fellowmen beside him, to the world and its order around him; next, that which brings him face to face with a Power to which he must bow, with a Providence which he must love and serve, with a being which he must adore—that which, in fine, gives man a doctrine to believe, a discipline to live by, and an object to worship. This is the ancient meaning of religion, and the fact of religion all over the world in every age. What is new in our scheme is merely that we avoid such terms as infinite, absolute, immaterial, and vague negatives altogether; resolutely confining ourselves to the sphere of what can be shown by experience, of what is relative and not absolute, and wholly and frankly *human*.

THE DEAN OF ST. PAUL'S.

IT seems to me difficult to discuss this question till it is settled, at least generally, what morality is influenced, and what religious belief is declining.

The morality generally acknowledged in Europe differs in most important points from that of the Hebrews in the days of Moses, of the Greeks in the days of Socrates, of the Romans under the Empire, of the monks of Egypt, of the Puritans of the seventeenth century. All of these had among them high types of character,—higher, it may be, than any types among us ; but who among us would accept their morality as a whole ? Our morality has come to be recognized as it is by a definite progress, of which the steps may be traced. It is plain that one form of religious thought and religious faith might aid this progress of morality by its decline, and another might, by its decline, impede or reverse it. On such a morality as we acknowledge, whencesoever derived, the decline of Buddhist belief or ancient Roman religious belief might act as a stimulus and a help. The decline of another kind of religious belief might, on the other hand, act most injuriously.

It seems to me, therefore, that till the question is presented in a concrete and historical form, nothing can be made of it. I do not understand the two terms of the comparison. Before I can attempt to answer it, I must know, at least approximately, *what* morality, and *what* religion.

·If by morality is meant the morality generally recog
nized in Europe, on the points of truthfulness, honesty,
humanity, purity, self-devotion, kindness, justice, fellow-
feeling,—and not only recognized, but judged by a conscious superiority of reason and experience to be the right
standard as compared with other moralities, such as those
of the Puritans, the monks, the Romans, the Hebrews,—
then I observe that as a matter of fact and history, which
to me seems incontrovertible, this morality has synchron-
ized in its growth and progress with an historical religion,
viz., Christianity.   We are come to the end of eighteen of
the most eventful and fruitful centuries of all, at least,
that are known to us; and we are landed in what we
accept as a purer morality than any which has been
known in the world before, and one which admits itself
not to be perfect, but contains in itself principles of im
provement and self-purification.   With this progress from
the first—sometimes, I quite admit, with gross and mischievous mistakes, but always with deliberate aim and
intention of good,—Christianity has been associated.
And in proportion as Christian religious belief has thrown
off additions not properly belonging to it, and has aimed
at its own purification and at a greater grasp of truth, the
standard and ideas of morality have risen with it.   The
difficulty at this moment is to determine how much of our
recognized morality, both directly and much more indirectly, has come from Christianity, and could not conceivably have come at all supposing Christianity absent.

I do not here, in these few lines, assume that in

Christianity and its long association with human morality, we have a *vera causa* of its improved and improving character. But with this immense fact of human experience before me, unique, it seems to me, in its kind, and in its broad outlines undeniable, no abstract reasonings can re-assure me as to the probability that with the failing powers of what has hitherto been, directly or indirectly, the source of much, and the support and sanction of still more, of our morality, our morality will fail too. It seems to me quite as easy to be sceptical about morality as it is about religion. If the religion has been proved to be not true, then of course it is no use talking about the matter. But if not, a declining belief in it may, with our present experience, be thought, at least by those who believe in it, to be attacking the roots of morality, if not in our own generation, at least in those which come after.

It is matter of history that in what we now generally accept as true morality, there are two factors : 1, On the one hand, human experience, human reasonableness, human good-feeling, human self-restraint; and (2) on the other, the belief, the laws, the ideas, the power of Christianity. It is difficult to conceive what reason there is to expect that if one factor is taken away the result will continue the same ; that the removal or weakening of such an important one as Christianity would not seriously affect such departments of morals as purity, the relations of the strong to the weak, respect for human life, slavery.

THE DUKE OF ARGYLL.

CONSIDERING that these papers are contributed by men belonging to very different schools of thought, and that they deal with a question very abstract and very ill-defined, it is surely very remarkable that so much agreement should· emerge on certain fundamental points.

Most remarkable of all in this respect, is the paper emanating from one of those who " follow the teaching of Comte."

In that paper I find the following propositions :

I. That morality is independent of theology ; but,

II. That it is not independent of religion, inasmuch as morality without religion cannot " suffice for life."

III. That religion means a scheme which (among other things), " brings man face to face with a Power to which he must bow, with a Providence which he must love and serve, with a Being which he must adore—that which, in fine, gives man a doctrine to believe, a discipline to live by, and an object to worship."

IV. That this scheme or conception of religion is "new," and differs from mere theology in the following distinctive points :

1. That it avoids certain words or phrases, such as "infinite," " absolute," " immaterial."

2. That it avoids also all " vague negatives."

3. That it resolutely confines us to the sphere of what

can be shown by experience—"of what is relative and not absolute," and "of what is wholly and frankly human."

I will examine these propositions in their order.

Proposition I. clearly depends entirely on what is meant by theology, and on the distinction which is drawn in the propositions which follow between theology and religion. Two things, however, may be said of this proposition : First, that, as a matter of historical fact, men's conceptions of moral obligation have been deeply influenced by their conceptions and beliefs about theology, or about the "whence and whither." Secondly, that as all branches of truth are and must be closely related to each other, it cannot possibly be true that morality is independent of theology, except upon the assumption that there is no truth in any theology. But this is an assumption which cannot be taken for granted, being very different indeed from the assumption (which may be reasonable), that no existing theology is unmixed with error. The absolute independence of morality as regards theology assumes much more than this ; it assumes that there is no theology containing even any important element of truth.

Proposition II. is, I think, perfectly true.

Proposition III. contains a definition of religion which might probably be accepted by any theological professor in any of our schools of divinity as good and true, if not in all respects adequate or complete.

Proposition IV. defines the elements in all theologies which constitute their fundamental errors, and which dis-

15

tinguish them from religion as defined in Proposition III. In short, Proposition III. defines affirmatively what religion is; and Proposition IV. defines negatively what it is not. It adds also a few more affirmative touches to complete the picture of what it is.

Looking now at the erroneous theological elements which are to be thrown away, we find three words fixed upon as specimens of what is vicious. One of them is "the Absolute." Most heartily do I wish it were abolished. More nonsense has been talked and written under cover of it than under cover of any other of the voluminous vocabulary of unintelligible metaphysics. It is admitted that the Absolute is "unthinkable," and things which are unthinkable had better be considered as also unspeakable, or at least be left unspoken.

Next "immaterial" is another word to be cast away. The worst of this demand is, that the words "material" and "immaterial" express a distinction of which we cannot get rid in thought. I do know that the pen with which I now write is made of that which to me is known as matter; but I do not know that the ideas which are expressed in this writing are made of any like substance, nor even of any substance like the brain. On the contrary, it seems to me that these ideas cannot be so made, and that there is an absolute difference between thought and the external substances which it thinks about. This may be my ignorance, but until that ignorance is removed I must accept those distinctions which are founded on the experience and observation of my own nature, and

I must retain words which are necessary to express them.

Then, as regards the word "infinite," in like manner, I cannot dispense with it, for the simple reason that the idea of infinity is one of which I cannot get rid, and which all science teaches me is an idea inseparable from our highest conception of the realities of Nature. Infinite time and infinite space, and the infinite duration of matter and of force, are conceptions which are part of my intellectual being, and I cannot "think them away." Metaphysicians may tell me that they are "forms of thought." But if so, they are at least all the more "frankly human," and I accept them as such.

Next we are to avoid "vague negatives altogether." Well, but surely a definition of religion as distinguished from theology, which consists in "avoiding" certain terms such as we have now examined, is a definition consisting of "vague negatives," and of nothing else.

But then we come next to an affirmative definition : " confining ourselves resolutely to the sphere of what can be shown by experience." To this I assent, provided experience be not confined to the sphere of sense, and provided everything which any man has ever felt, or known, or conceived, be accepted as in its own place and rank coming within the sphere which is thus described.

Again, it is demanded of us that we confine ourselves resolutely within " what is relative and not absolute." To this I assent. All knowledge is relative—both to the mind which knows, and relative also to all other things which remain to be known. Absolute goodness, and absolute power, and absolute knowledge, are all conceivable, but they are all relative ; and to talk of any object of knowledge, or of any subject of knowledge, as non-relative, is, or seems to me to be, simply nonsense.

Lastly, it is demanded of us to confine ourselves to what is "wholly and frankly human." If this means that we are not to think of any power or any being who is not related to our human faculties in a most definite and intelligible sense, I accept the limitation. But if it means that we are not to think of any such power or being except under all the imperfections, weaknesses, and vices of humanity, then the limitation is one which I cannot accept either as conceivable in itself, or as consistent with what I can see or understand of Nature.

But ought we not to be agreed in this ? If there is a Power to which man " must bow," " a Being which he must adore," and a " Providence which he must love and serve," it is clearly impossible that this Being, Power, or Providence can be " wholly human," in the sense of being no greater, no wiser, no better, than man himself.

The whole of this language is the language of theology and of nothing else—language, indeed, which may be held consistently with a vast variety of theological creeds, but which is inseparable from those fundamental conceptions which all such creeds involve, which is borrowed from them, and without which it has to me no intelligible sense.

With these explanations I accept the tenth paragraph of Paper No. IV., and that part of the last paragraph which has been already quoted, as expressing with admirable force and truth at least one aspect of the connection between morals and religion.

PROF. CLIFFORD.

IN the third of the preceding discourses there is so much which I can fully and fervently accept, that I should find it far more grateful to rest in that feeling of admiration and sympathy, then to attend to points of difference which seem to me to be of altogether secondary import. But for the truth's sake this must first be done, because it will then be more easy to point out some of the bearings of the position held in that discourse upon the question which is under discussion.

That the sense of duty in a man is the prompting of a self other than his own, is the very essence of it. Not only would morals not be self-sufficing if there were no such prompting of a wider self, but they could not exist; one might as well suppose a fire without heat. Not only is a sense of duty inherent in the constitution of our nature, but the prompting of a wider self than that of the individual is inherent in a sense of duty. It is no more possible to have the right without unselfishness, than to have man without a feeling for the right.

We may explain or account for these facts in various ways, but we shall not thereby alter the facts. No theories about heat and light will ever make a cold fire. And no doubt or disproof of any existing theory can any more extinguish that self other than myself, which speaks to me in the voice of conscience, than doubt or disproof of the wave-theory of light can put out the noonday sun.

One such theory is defended in the discourse here dealt with, and, if I may venture to say so, is not quite sufficiently distinguished from the facts which it is meant to explain. The theory is this: that the voice of conscience in my mind is the voice of a conscious being external to me and to all men, who has made us and all the world. When this theory is admitted, the observed discrepancy between our moral sense and the government of the world, as a whole, makes it necessary to suppose another world and another life in it for men, whereby this discord shall be resolved in a final harmony.

I fully admit that the theistic hypothesis, so grounded, and considered apart from objections otherwise arising, is a reasonable hypothesis and an explanation of the facts. The idea of an external conscious being is unavoidably suggested, as it seems to me, by the categorical imperative of the moral sense; and, moreover, in a way quite independent, by the aspect of Nature, which seems to answer to our questionings with an intelligence akin to our own. It is more reasonable to assume one consciousness than two, if by that one assumption we can explain two distinct facts; just as if we had been led to assume an ether to explain light and an ether to explain electricity, we might have run before experiment and guessed that these two ethers were but one. But since there is a discordance between Nature and conscience, the theory of their common origin in a mind external to humanity has not met with such acceptance as that of the divine origin of each. A large number of theists have rejected it, and taken refuge in Manichæism and the doctrine of the Demiurgus in various forms; while others have endeavoured, as aforesaid, to redress the balance of the old world by calling into existence a new one.

It is, however, a very striking and significant fact, that the very great majority of mankind who have thought about these questions at all, while acknowledging the existence of divine beings and their influence in the government of the world, have sought for the spring and sanction of duty in something above and beyond the gods. The religions of Brahmanism and of Buddhism, and the moral system of Confucius, have together ruled over more than two-thirds of the human race during the historic period: and in all of these the moral sense is regarded as arising indeed out of a universal principle, but not as personified in any conscious being. This vast body of dissent might well, it should seem, make us ask if there is anything unsatisfying in the theory which represents the voice of conscience as the voice of a god.

Although, as I have said, the idea of an external conscious being is unavoidably suggested by the moral sense, yet, if this idea should be found untrue, it does not follow that Nature has been fooling us. The idea is not in the facts, but in our inference from the facts. A mirror unavoidably suggests the idea of a room behind it; but it is not our eyes that deceive us, it is only the inference we draw from their testimony. Further consideration may lead to a different inference of far greater practical value.

Now, whether or no it be reasonable and satisfying to the conscience, it cannot be doubted that theistic belief is a comfort and a solace to those who hold it, and that the loss of it is a very painful loss. It cannot be doubted, at least by many of us in this generation, who either profess it now, or received it in our childhood and have parted from it since with such searching trouble as only cradle-faiths can cause. We have seen the spring sun shine out of an empty heaven, to light up a soulless earth; we have felt with utter loneliness that the Great Companion is dead. Our children, it may be hoped, will know that sorrow only by the reflex light of a wondering compassion. But to say that theistic belief is a comfort and a solace, and to say that it is the crown or coping of morality, these are different things.

For in what way shall belief in God strengthen my sense of duty? *He is a great one working for the right.* But I already know so many, and I know these so well. *His righteousness is unfathomable; it transcends all ideals.* But I have not yet fathomed the goodness of living men whom I know; still less of those who have lived, and whom I know. And the goodness of all these is a striving

for something better; now it is not the goal, but the
striving for it, that matters to me. The essence of their
goodness is the losing of the individual self in another
and a wider self; but God cannot do this; his goodness
must be something different. *He is infinitely great and
powerful, and he lives forever.* I do not understand this
mensuration of goodness by foot-pounds, and seconds, and
cubic miles. A little field-mouse, which busies itself in
the hedge, and does not mind my company, is more to
me than the longest ichthyosaurus that ever lived, even if
he lived a thousand years. When we look at a starry
sky, the spectacle whose awfulness Kant compared with
that of the moral sense, does it help out our poetic emotion to reflect that these specks are really very very big,
and very very hot, and very very far away ? Their heat
and their bigness oppress us; we should like them to be
taken still farther away, the great blazing lumps. But
when we think of the unseen planets that surround
them, of the wonders of life, of reason, of love, that may
dwell therein, then indeed there is something sublime in
the sight. Fitness and kinship: these are the truly great
things for us, not force and massiveness and length of
days.

Length of days, said the old rabbi, is measured not by
their number, but by the work that is done in them. We
are all to be swept away in the final ruin of the earth.
The thought of that ending is a sad thought; there is no
use in trying to deny this. But it has nothing to do with
right and wrong; it belongs to another subject. Like

All-father Odin, we must ride out gayly to do battle with the wolf of doom, even if there be no Balder to come back and continue our work. At any rate the right will have been done; and the past is safer than all store-houses.

The conclusion of the matter is, that belief in God and in a future life is a source of refined and elevated pleasure to those who can hold it. But the foregoing of a refined and elevated pleasure, because it appears that we have no right to indulge in it, is not in itself, and cannot produce a^s its consequence, a decline of morality.

There is another theory of the facts of the moral sense set forth in the succeeding discourse, and this seems to me to be the true one. The voice of conscience is the voice of our father-man who is within us; the accumulated instinct of the race is poured into each one of us, and overflows us, as if the ocean were poured into a cup.[1] Our evidence for this explanation is that the cause assigned is a *vera causa*; it undoubtedly exists; there is no *perhaps* about that. And those who have tried tell us that it is sufficient; the explanation, like the fact, " covers the whole voluntary field." The lightest and the gravest action may be consciously done in and for man. And the sympathetic aspect of Nature is explained to us in the same way. In so far as our conception of Nature is akin to our minds that conceive it, man made it; and man made us, with the necessity to conceive it in this way.[2]

---

[1] Schopenhauer. There is a most remarkable article on the "Natural History of Morals" in the *North British Review*, December, 1867.

[2] For an admirable exposition of the doctrine of the social origin of our conceptions, *see* Prof. Croom Robertson's paper, " How we come by our Knowledge," in the first number of *The Nineteenth Century*.

I do not, however, suppose that morality would practically gain much from the wide acceptance of true views about its nature, except in a way which I shall presently suggest. I neither admit the moral influence of theism in the past, nor look forward to the moral influence of humanism in the future. Virtue is a habit, not a sentiment or an -ism. The doctrine of total depravity seems to have been succeeded by a doctrine of partial depravity, according to which there is hope for human affairs, but still men cannot go straight unless some tremendous, all-embracing theory has a finger in the pie. Theories are most important and excellent things when they help us to see the matter as it really is, and so to judge what is the right thing to do in regard to it. They are the guides of action, but not the springs of it. Now the springs of virtuous action is the social instinct, which is set to work by the practice of comradeship. The union of men in a common effort for a common object—*band-work*, if I may venture to translate coöperation into English—this is, and always has been, the true school of character. Except in times of severe struggle for national existence, the practice of virtue by masses of men has always been coincident with municipal freedom, and with the vigour of such unions as are not large enough to take from each man his conscious share in the work and in the direction of it.

What really affects morality is not religious belief, but a practice which, in some times and places, is thought to be religious—namely, the practice of submitting human life to clerical control. The apparent destructive tendency

of modern times, which arouses fear and foreboding of
evil in the minds of many of the best of men, seems to me
to be not mainly an intellectual movement. It has its intellectual side, but that side is the least important, and
touches comparatively few souls. The true core of it is
a firm resolve of men to know the right at first hand,
which has grown out of the strong impulse given to the
moral sense by political freedom. Such a resolve is a
necessary condition to the existence of a pure and noble
theism like that of the third discourse, which learns what
God is like by thinking of man's love for man. Although
that doctrine has been prefigured and led up to for many
ages by the best teaching of Englishmen, and—what is
far more important—by the best practice of Englishmen,
yet it cannot be accepted on a large scale without what
will seem to many a decline of religious belief. For assuredly if men learn the nature of God from the moral
sense of man, they cannot go on believing the doctrines
of popular theology. Such change of belief is of small
account in itself, for any consequences it can bring about;
but it is of vast importance as a symptom of the increasing power and clearness of the sense of duty.

On the other hand, there is one "decline of religious
belief," inseparable from a revolution in human conduct,
which would indeed be a frightful disaster to mankind.
A revival of any form of sacerdotal Christianity would
be a matter of practice and not a matter of theory. The
system which sapped the foundation of patriotism in the
old world; which well nigh eradicted the sense of intel-

lectual honesty, and seriously weakened the habit of truth-speaking, which lowered men's reverence for the marriage-bond by placing its sanctions in a realm outside of Nature instead of in the common life of men, and by the institutions of monasticism and a celibate clergy ; which stunted the moral sense of the nations by putting a priest between every man and his conscience—this system, if it should ever return to power, must be expected to produce worse evils than those which it has worked in the past. The house which it has once made desolate has been partially swept and garnished by the free play gained for the natural goodness of men. It would come back accompanied by social diseases perhaps worse than itself, and the wreck of civilized Europe would be darker than the darkest of past ages.

DR. WARD.

I AGREE with the Dean of St. Paul's, that the wording of our question is unfortunately ambiguous; and I think that this fact has made the discussion in several respects less pointed and less otherwise interesting than it might have been.

For my present purpose, I understand the term " religious belief" as including essentially belief in a personal God and in personal immortality. Less than this is not worthy the name of religious belief; and, on the other hand, I will not refer to any other religious truths than these. I am to inquire, therefore, what would be the influence on morality of a decline in these two beliefs.

But next, what is meant by "morality?" I will explain, as clearly as brevity may permit, what I should myself understand by the term; though I am, of course, well aware that this is by no means the sense in which Sir J. Fitzjames Stephen, or Mr. Harrison, or Prof. Clifford, understands it.

I consider that there is a certain authoritative rule of life,[1] necessarily not contingently existing, which may be regarded under a twofold aspect. It declares that certain acts (exterior or interior) are intrinsically and necessarily evil; it declares, again, that some certain act (exterior or interior), even where not actually evil, is by intrinsic necessity, under the circumstances of some given moment, less morally excellent than some certain other act. Any given man, therefore, more effectively practises "morality," in proportion as he more energetically, predominantly, and successfully aims at adjusting his whole conduct, interior and exterior, by this authoritative rule. Accordingly, when I am asked what is the bearing of some particular influence on morality, I understand myself to be asked how far such influence affects for good or evil the prevalence of that practical habit which I have just described; how far such influence disposes men (or the contrary) to adjust their conduct by this authoritative rule.

---

[1] To prevent misapprehension I may explain that, in my view, those various necessary truths which collectively constitute this rule are, like all other necessary truths, founded on the essence of God; they are what they are because he is what he is.

These explanations having been premised, my answer to the proposed question is this : The absence of religious belief—of a belief in a personal God and personal immortality—does not simply *injure* morality, but, if the disbelievers carry their view out consistently, utterly *destroys* it. I affirm—which, of course, requires proof, though I have no space here to give it—that no one except a theist can, in consistency, recognize the necessarily existing authoritative rule of which I have spoken. But for practical purposes there is no need of this affirmation, because in what follows I shall refer to no other opponents of religion, except that antitheistic body—consisting of agnostics, positivists, and the like—which in England just now heads the speculative irreligious movement. .Now, it is manifest on the very surface of philosophical literature that, as *a matter of fact*, these men deny in theory the existence of any such necessary authoritative rule as that on which I have dwelt. A large proportion of theists accept it, and call it " the Natural Law ;"[1] an agnostic or positivist denies its existence. It is very clear that he who denies that there is such a thing as a necessarily existing authoritative rule of life cannot consistently aim at adjusting any, even the smallest, part of his conduct by the intimations of that rule ; or, in other words, cannot

---

[1] The Natural Law more strictly includes only God's *prohibition* of acts intrinsically evil, and his *preception* of acts which cannot be omitted *without* doing what is intrinsically evil. But we may with obvious propriety so extend the term as to include under it God's *counselling* of those acts which, as clothed in their full circumstances, are by intrinsic necessity the more morally excellent.

consistently do so much as one act which (on the theory which I follow) can be called morally good.

Here, however, a most important explanation must be made. It continually happens that some given philosopher holds some given doctrine speculatively and theoretically, while he holds the precisely contradictory doctrine implicitly and unconsciously; inasmuch that it is the latter, and not the former, which he applies to his estimate of events as they successively arise. Now the existence of the Natural Law—so I would most confidently maintain—is a truth so firmly rooted by God himself in the conviction of every reasonable creature, that practically to leaven the human mind with belief of its contradictory is, even under the circumstances most favourable to that purpose, a slow and up-hill process. In the early stages, therefore, of antitheistic persuasion, there is a vast gulf between the antitheist's speculative theory and his practical realization of that theory. Mr. Mallock has set forth this fact, I think, with admirable force, in an article contributed by him to the *Contemporary* of last January. When antitheists say—such is his argument—that the pursuit of truth is a " sacred," " heroic," " noble " exercise —when they call one way of living mean, and base, and hateful, and another way of living great, and blessed, and admirable—they are guilty of most flagrant inconsistency. They therein use language and conceive thoughts which are utterly at variance with their own speculative theory. If it be admitted (1) that the idea expressed by the term " moral goodness " is a simple idea, an idea incapable of analysis; and (2) that to this idea there corresponds a necessary objective reality *in rerum natura*—if these two propositions be admitted, the existence of the Natural Law is a truth which irresistibly results from the admission. On the other hand, if these two propositions be *not* postulated, then to talk of one human act being "higher" or "nobler" than another is as simply unmeaning as to talk of a bed being nobler than a chair, or a plough than a harrow. Whether it be the bed, or the plough, or the human act, it may be more *useful* than the other article with which it is brought into comparison; but to speak in either case of "nobleness" is as the sound of a tinkling cymbal. Or rather, which is my present point, the fact of antitheists using such language shows that their practical belief is so far essentially opposed and (as I, of course, should say) immeasurably superior to their speculative theory. To my mind there is hardly any truth which needs more to be insisted on than this, in the present crisis of philosophical thought: when antitheism successfully conceals its hideous deformity from its own votaries, by dressing itself up in the very garments of that rival creed which it derides as imbecile and obsolete. I heartily wish I had space for setting forth in full and clear light the argument on which I would here insist. I may refer, however, to Mr. Mallock's article, for an excellent exposition of it from his own point of view; and, in particular, I cannot express too strongly my concurrence with the following remarks:

" All the moral feelings " (he says) " at present afloat in the world

16

depend, as I have already shown, on the primary doctrines of religion ; but that the former would *outlive* the latter is nothing more than we should naturally expect ; just as water may go on boiling after it is taken off the fire, as flowers keep their scent and colour after we have plucked them, or as a tree whose roots have been cut may yet put out green leaves for one spring more. But a time must come when all this will be over, and when the true effects of what has been done will begin to show themselves. Nor can there be any reason brought forward to show why, if the creed of unbelief was once fully assented to by the world, all morality—a thing always attended by some pain and struggle—would not gradually wither away, and give place to a more or less successful seeking after pleasure, no matter of what kind."

I would also recall to Sir J. Fitzjames Stephen's remembrance an admirable statement of his, which occurred in the work on ' Liberty, Equality, and Fraternity." " We cannot judge of the effects of atheism," he says, " from the conduct of persons who have been educated as believers in God, and in the midst of a nation which believes in God. If we should ever see a generation of men, especially a generation · of Englishmen, to whom the word ' God' has no meaning at all, we should get a light on the subject which might be lurid enough."[1]

So far I have used the word " morality " in that sense which I account the true one. But a different acceptation of the word is very common ; and it will be better perhaps briefly to consider our proposed question in the sense which that acceptation would give it. Morality, then, is often spoken of as consisting in a man's sacrifice of his

---

[1] Second edition, p. 326.

personal desires for the public good; so that each man more faithfully practises " morality " in proportion as he more effectively postpones private interests to public ones. I have always been extremely surprised that any theist can use this terminology; though I am well aware, of course, that many do so.   To mention no other of its defects, it excludes ¦from the sphere of morality precisely what a theist must consider the most noble and elevating branch thereof, viz., men's duties to their Creator.   Constant rememberance of God's presence, prayer to him for moral strength, purging the heart from any such wordly attachment as may interfere with his sovereignty over the affections—these, and a hundred others, which are man's highest moral actions, are excluded by this strange terminology from being moral actions at all.   Still, in one respect there is great agreement between the two "moralities" in question, for under either of them morality very largely consists in self-denial and self-sacrifice.

Now, if it be asked in what way morality, as so understood, would be affected by the absence of religious belief, I think the true reply is one which has so often been drawn out that I need do no more than indicate it. Firstly, apart from theistic motives there is no sufficient moral leverage; men would not have the moral strength required for sustained self-denial and self-sacrifice. Secondly and more importantly, if theistic sanctions were away, no theory could be drawn out explaining why it should be *reasonable* that a man sacrifice his personal interest to that of his fellows.

On this matter I am glad that I have the opportunity
of drawing attention to a very fine passage of Mr.
Goldwin Smith's, published in the *Macmillan* of last
January :[1]

"Materialism has, in fact, already begun to show its effects on
human conduct and on society. They may perhaps be more visible
in communities where social conduct depends greatly on individual
conviction and motive than in communities which are more ruled by
tradition and bound together by strong class organizations though
the decay of morality will perhaps be more complete and disastrous
in the latter than in the former. God and future retribution being
out of the question, it is difficult to see what can restrain the selfishness of an ordinary man, and induce him, in the absence of actual coercion, to sacrifice his personal desires to the public good.
The service of humanity is the sentiment of a refined mind conver-
sant with history ; within no calculable time is it likely to overrule
the passions and direct the conduct of the mass. And after all,
without God or spirit, what is 'humanity?' One school of science
reckons a hundred and fifty different species of man. What is the
bond of unity between all these species, and wherein consists the
obligation to mutual love and help ? A zealous servant of science
told Agassiz that the age of real civilization would have begun when
you could go out and shoot a man for scientific purposes ; and in the
controversy respecting the Jamaica massacre we had proof enough
that the ascendancy of science and a strong sense of human brotherhood might be very different things. 'Apparent diræ facies.' We
begin to perceive, looming through the mist, the lineaments of an
epoch of selfishness compressed by a government of force."

In fact, even in the present early stage of English antitheistic philosophy, if its adherents are directly asked what

is man's reasonable rule of life, I know of no other answer they will theoretically give except one. They will say that any given person's one reasonable pursuit on earth is to aim at his own earthly happiness—to obtain for himself out of life the greatest amount he can of gratification No doubt they will make confident statements on the indissoluble connections between happiness and "virtue." Still, according to their speculative theory, the only reasonable ground for practising "virtue" is its conduciveness to the agent's happiness.

Now, let us suppose a generation to grow up, profoundly imbued with this principle, carrying it consistently into detail, emancipated from the unconscious influence of (what I must be allowed to call) a more respectable creed. What would be the result ? Evidently a man so trained, in calculating for himself the balance of pleasure and pain, will give no credit on the former side to such gratifications as might arise from consciousness of conquest over his lower nature, or from the pursuit of lofty and generous aims. These, I say, will have no place in his list of pleasures : because he will have duly learned his lesson, that there is no "lower" or "higher" nature ; that no one aim can be "loftier" than any other; that there is nothing more admirable in generosity than in selfishness. On the other hand, neither will he include, under his catalogue of *pains*, any feeling of remorse for evil committed, or any dread of possible punishment in some future life ; for he will look with simple contempt on those doctrines, which are required as the foundation for such pains. His common-sense course will be to make this world as comfortable a place as he can, by bringing every possible prudential calculation to bear on his purpose. Before all things, he will keep his digestion in good order. He will keep at arms'-length (indeed at many arms'-lengths) every disquieting consideration, such, e. g., as might arise from a remembrance of other men's misery, or from a thought of that repulsive spectre which the superstitious call moral obligation.

It is plain that duly to pursue the subject thus opened would carry me indefinitely beyond my limits ;[1] and I will only, therefore, make one concluding observation. If the term "virtue" be retained by those of whom I am speaking, it will be used, I suppose to express any habitual practice which solidly conduces to the agent's balance of earthly enjoyment. I am confident that—should this be the recognized terminology, and should the new school be permitted to arrive at its legitimate development—there is one habit which would be very prominent among its catalogue of "virtues." The habit to which I refer is indulgence in licentiousness—licentiousness practised, no doubt, prudently, discreetly, calculatingly, but at the same time habitually, perseveringly, and with keen zest.

[1] I have treated at somewhat greater length in an article which I contributed to the *Dublin Review* of January, 1877, pp. 15-21.

PROF. HUXLEY.

W E are led to do this thing, and to avoid that, partly by instinct and partly by conscious motives; and our conduct is said to be moral or the reverse, partly on the ground of its effects upon other beings, partly upon that of its operation upon ourselves.

Social morality relates to that course of action which tends to increase the happiness or diminish the misery of other beings; personal morality relates to that which has the like effect upon ourselves.

If this be so, the foundation of morality must needs lie in the constitution of Nature, and must depend on the mental construction of ourselves and of other sentient beings.

The constitution of man remaining what it is, his capacity for the pleasures and pains afforded by sense, by sympathy, or by the contemplation of moral beauty and ugliness, is obviously in no way affected by the abbreviation or the prolongation of his conscious life; nor by the mere existence or non-existence of anything not included in Nature; nor, so long as he believes that actions have consequences, does it matter to him what connection there may be between these actions and other phenomena of Nature.

The assertion that morality is any way dependent upon the views respecting certain philosophical problems a person may chance to hold, produces the same effect upon my mind as if one should say that a man's vision depends on his theory of light; or that he has no business to be sure that ginger is hot in the mouth unless he has formed definite views, in the first place, as to the nature of ginger, and, secondly, as to whether he has or has not a sensitive soul

Social morality belongs to the realm of inductive and deductive investigation. Given a society of human beings under certain circumstances: and the question whether a particular action on the part of one of the members of that society will tend to the increase of the general happiness or not is a question of natural knowledge, and, as such, is a perfectly legitimate subject of scientific inquiry. And the morality or immorality of the action will depend upon the answer which the question receives.

If it can be shown, by observation or experiment, that theft, murder, and adultery, do not tend to diminish the happiness of society, then, in the absence of any but natural knowledge, they are not social immoralities.

It does not follow, however, that they might not be personal immoralities. Without committing myself to any theory of the origin of the moral sense, or even as to the existence of any such special sense, I may suggest that it is quite conceivable that discords and harmonies may affect the congeries of feelings to which we give the name, as they do others.

I see no reason for doubting that the beauty of holiness and the ugliness of sin are, to a great many minds, no mere metaphors, but feelings as real and as intense as those with which the beauty or ugliness of form or colour fills the artist-mind, and that they are as independent of intellectual beliefs, and even of education, as are all the true æsthetic powers and impulses.

On the other hand, I do not doubt the existence of persons, like the hero of the "Fatal Boots," devoid of any sense of moral beauty or ugliness, and for them personal morality has no existence. They may offend, but they cannot sin; they may be sorry for having stolen or murdered, because society punishes them for their social immoralities, but they are incapable of repentance.

Before going further, I think it may be needful to discriminate between religion and theology.

I object to the very general use of the terms religion and theology, as if they were synonymous, or indeed had anything whatever to do with one another. Religion is the affair of the affections, theology of the intellect. The religious man loves an ideal perfection, which may be natural or non-natural; the theologian expounds the attributes of what he terms "supernatural." Being as so many scientific truths, the consequences of which work into the general scheme of Nature, and are there discernible by ordinary methods of investigation. What the theologian affirms may be put in this way: that beyond the *natura naturata*, mirrored or made by the natural operations of the human mind, there is a *natura naturans*, sufficient knowledge of which is attainable only through the channel of revelation.

Now, I think it cannot be doubted that both religion

and theology, as thus defined, have exercised, and must exercise, a profound influence on morality. For it may be that the object of a man's religion—the ideal which he worships—is an ideal of sensual enjoyment, or of domination, or of the development of all his faculties toward perfection, or of self-annihilation, or of benevolence; and his personal morality will, in part, contribute largely to the formation of his ideal, and will, in part, be swayed and bent until it harmonizes with that ideal.

Moreover, it is clear that a man's theology may give him such views of the action of the *natura naturans* as will profoundly modify or even reverse his social morality.

He may see ground for believing that conduct of evil effect upon society, which is part of the *natura naturata*, is in harmony with the laws of action of the *natura naturans;* and that, as the rewards and punishments of men are but slight and temporary, while those inflicted by the greater power behind the *natura naturata*, are grievous and endless, common prudence may dictate obedience to the stronger. And history proves that there is no social crime that man can commit which has not been dictated by theology and committed on theological grounds. On the other hand, the belief that the divine commands are identical with the laws of social morality has lent infinite strength to the latter in all ages.

In like manner it seems to me impossible to over-estimate the influence of speculative beliefs as to the nature of the Deity, apart from all idea of rewards and punishments, upon personal morality. The lover of moral beauty, struggling through a world full of sorrow and sin, is surely as much the stronger for believing that sooner or later a vision of perfect peace and goodness will burst upon him, as the toiler up a mountain for the belief that beyond crag and snow lie home and rest. For the other side of the picture, who shall exaggerate the deadly influence on personal morality of those theologies which have represented the Deity as vain-glorious, irritable, and revengeful—as a sort of pedantic drill-sergeant of mankind, to whom no valour, no long-tried loyalty, could atone for the misplacement of a button of the uniform, or the misunderstanding of a paragraph of the " regulations and instructions ?"

While no one can dare history, or even look about him, without admitting the enormous influence of theology on morality, it would perhaps be hard to say whether it has been greater or less than the influence of morality on theology. But the latter topic is not at present under discussion ; and the only further remark I would venture to add is this—that the intensity and reality of the action of theological beliefs upon morality are precisely measured by the conviction of those who hold them that they are true. That such and such a doctrine conduces to morality, and disbelief in it to immorality, may be demonstrated by an endless array of convincing syllogisms ; but, unless the doctrine is true, the practical result of this expenditure of logic is not apparent. I have not the slightest doubt that if mankind could be got to believe that every socially immoral act would be instantly followed by three months' severe toothache, such acts would soon cease to be perpetrated. It would be a faith charged with most beneficent works, but unfortunately this faith can so easily be shown to be disaccordant with fact that it is not worth while to become its prophet.

For my part I do not for one moment admit that morality is not strong enough to hold its own. But if it is demonstrated to me that I am wrong, and that without this or that theological dogma the human race will lapse into bipedal cattle, more brutal than the beasts by the measure of their greater cleverness, my next question is to ask for the proof of the truth of the dogma.

If this proof is forthcoming, it is my conviction that no drowning sailor ever clutched a hen-coop more tenaciously than mankind will hold by such dogma, whatever it may be. But if not, then I verily believe that the human race will go its evil way; and my only consolation lies in the reflection that, however bad our posterity may become, so long as they hold by the plain rule of not pretending to believe what they have no reason to believe because it may be to their advantage so to pretend, they will not have reached the lowest depths of immorality.

MR. R. H. HUTTON.

THAT has happened to us which happened to the disputants in that Attic Symposium from which, I suppose, the name for our discussion was taken. We have been interrupted by a " great knocking at the door " and the entrance of an unbidden guest, who, however, shows no sign either of Alcibiades's intoxication, or of that generous disposition to crown the most deserving with garlands which may perhaps have had some connection with the excesses of the brilliant Athenian's potations. The *Saturday Reviewer*, who, without dropping his mask, has thrust upon us his own criticism on our discussion,[1] has certainly not conferred the most meagre of wreaths on any one, unless indeed it may be said that he grudgingly crowns the Dean of St. Paul's and the Duke of Argyll with a withered sprig or two of parsley, for pointing out that our subject is much too vague, and for trying to narrow a discussion so " abstract and ill-defined." His general criticism is contained in the harsh remark that " all the fine talk of the chosen *illuminati* is a mass of words with very little meaning," and that " the deliberations of the Symposium bear a very strong resemblance to those of the diplomatists who have been lately concocting protocols ; that is, they consist of empty phrases to which all the parties can agree because they do not

---

[1] See *Saturday Review* for March 31, 1877. Article, " A Modern Symposium."

touch any of the points on which the co-signataries would be likely to differ." That is a much crueler interruption than any caused by Alcibiades to the guests assembled at the Symposium of Plato, nor do I think it is quite just, though there is enough justice in it to make me try to bring out what seem to me the clearly-understood issues between us a little more distinctly, in the few words I have to say. To limit the subject as much as possible, I will speak of nothing but the effect likely to be produced on morality by any decline in the belief in a righteous God independent of, and external to, the human race— in one, that is, whose leading purpose in relation to us is believed to be to mould our motives and characters into the likeness of his own. Now it seems to me that all the previous speakers except two, Mr. Frederic Harrison and Prof. Clifford, believe, for different reasons, and in different degrees, that such a decline in such a belief in God would probably result in a parallel decline in human morality; though some insist most, like Sir James Stephen and Prof. Huxley, on the point that any attempt to bolster up the belief artificially *for the sake* of its moral consequences, by discountenancing free discussion, would result in a worse decline of morality, and others insist most, like Dr. Martineau, Lord Selborne, and Dean Church, on the point that the same causes which result in a decline in this belief (especially as it is represented in Christianity) are likely to result also in a decline in the force of the ethical principles so closely associated with it. But I do not understand any one to differ with

Prof. Huxley, that if the belief can be shown to be false, be the moral consequence what it may, it ought to go. On the other hand, I understand both Mr. Harrison and Prof. Clifford to assert that the causes which, as they think, have undermined and are undermining the belief in a righteous God, external to the human race, have no tendency to undermine the binding power of the highest human ethics, but, on the contrary, have a direct tendency to elevate and refine them, though Prof. Clifford regards this tendency as, on the whole, slight, and confined chiefly to the blow which such a change in belief will have in diminishing the control of the clergy, while Mr. Harrison expects very much indeed from it, if only through its tendency to concentrate on the desirable aims of a real world, an enthusiasm now so much dissipated in his opinion, by lavishing it on imaginary objects.

Now, while I heartily admit with Prof. Huxley the conceivability that a gross delusion—like the belief that "every socially immoral act would instantly be followed by three months' severe toothache"—if it could be palmed off successfully upon our race, would have *some* very beneficial consequences—(some, also, by no means beneficial) —and should not a bit the less regard a conspiracy, even if one were practicable, to impose such a delusion on our race, as a great sin, I cannot the more on that account see how to disentangle the question whether there be a righteous God external to men from the question whether there would be a great moral loss to human nature in the dissipation of the belief in such a God. It is quite con-

ceivable—nay, it has often happened—that a sincere delusion has produced the best results. The belief in an
imaginary danger of death, for instance, has often made
a man take life more seriously; and the belief in an
imaginary danger of invasion has probably often bound
a divided nation together and given it a greater nervous
strength and manliness. But though it is easy to conceive a belief, in some respects beneficial, which is wholly
false, it seems to me, in the case before us, that the very
element in the belief we are discussing, which makes it
beneficial, is also a clear note of its truth. What makes
the belief in such a God as I have spoken of beneficial is
that this belief, and this only, gives to the attitude of man's
mind, in relation to right motive and right action, that
mixture of courage and cheerful irresponsibility for the
result characteristic of a *faith*. Luther's great saying,
" We say to our Lord God that if he will have his Church,
he must uphold it, for we cannot uphold it, and, even if
we could, we should become the proudest asses under
heaven,"[1] would be of course simply untranslatable into
any humanist or positivist dialect at all. I do not indeed
quite know what Mr. Harrison means when he talks of a
" frankly human " religion which shall provide us with
a " Providence " whom we are " to love and serve ;" but
I suppose he must mean that we are to love that law of
the universe which produces a certain amount of correspondence between our nature and its " environment,"

---

[1] " Tischreden," edition Förstemaun, Leipsic, 1844, vol. ii., p. 330.

and that we are to coöperate with that law. At least
this is the only meaning I am able to attach to "loving
and serving" a Providence without believing in God.
Now for myself I am incapable of loving a mere law of
any kind, whether it be a law of gravitation, a law of
assimilation between my organism and its environment,
or any other ; and as for "serving" it, I like to judge for
myself, and, instead of allowing myself always to be
assimilated to my "environment," I sometimes prefer
what is called, in the language of the same philosophy,
"differentiating" myself from it. But I think even Mr.
Harrison would hardly justify language of trust like
Luther's, toward a "Being" of whom we are supposed to
know nothing except that it has given rise to the earth
we live on, and will most likely, in a few thousand years,
also put a final end to it. You cannot trust a being of
whose purposes, or capacity for having purposes, you
know nothing, because trust implies approving those
purposes and believing them to be accompanied by a far
higher range of knowledge and foresight than your own.
Yet has not all the benefit of trust in God arisen from that
humility and courage, that self-abandonment to a higher
will, that sense of complete irresponsibility for the result
when the right thing is once done, which constitute moral
heroism ?   Could such moral heroism sustain the belief
in a divine will which is shaping all right action to a perfect end ? Suppose we believed in unknown causes which
produce indeed such moral phenomena as those of human
life for a moment in the long ages of evolution—which

17

bring them like a ripple to the surface, but quench them, like that ripple, for evermore, and which are as certain so to quench them as the sun is one day to be burned out—is it possible we could cast ourselves on such unknown causes with the sort of faith in God that has "moved mountains," and that will move mountains again that will say, for instance, to this huge dead weight of secularism and positivism, "Be thou cast into the sea," and it will obey ?

Nor can I see any better help in Prof. Clifford's substitute for God—namely, the higher self represented by "the voice of our Father Man who is within us," i.e., by "the accumulated instinct of the race poured into each one of us" and overflowing us, "as if the ocean were poured into a cup." The "accumulated instinct of our race" includes a great deal of evil as well as good, and is often unaccompanied by any accumulation of instinct for the suppressing of the evil by the good. I quite agree with those who have urged that it was the "accumulated instinct" of the Athenian people which taught them the necessity of putting down Socrates as one who was undermining the social order to which he belonged. I do not doubt that Socrates shared that accumulated instinct not less—nay, probably much more—than the rest of his countrymen. Probably it overflooded him "as an ocean might overflow a cup." Nevertheless the solitary voice within him, which he attributed to his "dæmon," though it could not drown the voice of this "accumulated instinct," was heard above it, and prevailed over the pleas of comradeship, and over what Prof. Clifford deems the only "spring of virtuous action," the impulse which invites men to make individual sacrifices to promote the greater efficiency of the social bond.

"Some one may wonder (says Socrates, in Plato's Apology) why I go about in private giving advice and busying myself with the concerns of others, but do not venture to come forward in public and advise the state.   I will tell you the reason of this.   You have often heard me speak of an oracle or sign which comes to me, and is the divinity which Meletus ridicules in the indictment.   This sign I have had ever since I was a child.   The sign is a voice which comes to me and always forbids me to do something which I am going to do, but never commands me to do anything, and this is what stands in the way of my being a politician.   And rightly, as I think.   For I am certain, O men of Athens, that if I had engaged in politics I should have perished long ago, and done no good either to you or to myself.   And don't be afraid of my telling you the truth, for the truth is that no man who goes to war with you or any other multitude, honestly struggling against the commission of unrighteousness and wrong in the state, will save his life ; he will really fight for the right, if he would live even for a little while, must have a private station and not a public one."[1]

This is unsocial doctrine enough, and, of course, Prof. Clifford will say that, though fatal to the existing Athenian state, it had its source in instincts essential to a higher political virtue and to the cohesion of a nobler kind of state.   Grant it for a moment.   Yet how can we expect moral heroism of the same type as that which is convinced that invisible Power is on its side, and trusts to

---

[1] Prof. Jowett's " Plato," vol. i., p. 346, first edition,

the vindication of the future, if instead of ascribing the origin of its impulses to a divine power which is the same yesterday, to-day and forever—a power above it and beyond it—he who has to evince this moral heroism believes that there is no inspiring mind higher than his own, and holds, therefore, that he must rely on himself, and on himself alone, for the fine faculty to discriminate between the inchoate order of a new society and the worn-out guarantees of an order which is passing away? How is one who is fully aware that he is dissolving the ancient bonds of a venerable society and polity, but who only *hopes* that he is creating the germs of something better, to set his face against the brotherhood among whom he lives, and to defy the wrath of the fellow-citizens whom he sees, and all without the whisper of approval from any spiritual being behind the veil? Surely the hesitating inspiration of that long-buried ancestor, " our Father Man "—to admit, for a moment, Prof. Clifford's assumption—when it spells out dubious and unaccustomed lessons which the voices of our brother-men join, in loud chorus, to decry, would not be very likely to triumph over fears and scruples which " our Father Man " also authenticates, and authenticates much more positively than he ever can authenticate the first faintly uttered principles of a new kind of social union against the old. What was it, as I asked before, which stimulated Luther to his gigantic enterprise? Not the doubtful guess that buried generations had transmitted to him the glimpse of a reform which would transfigure society, but the belief that he could honestly use the language of that psalm that he so much delighted to appropriate to himself: "They came about me like bees, and are extinct even as the fire among the thorns, for in the name of the Lord I will destroy them." Whether the belief in "our Father Man" and in a tentative Providence which does not *foresee*, but only accommodates the individual to his "environment," as the only guides of our moral life, be wild or sober, this, I think, is clear, that it does not provide the martyr or the reformer with the stimulating power of a *faith ;* that it can give no confidence like that in an inspiration of far wider grasp and far deeper purpose than any which the reformer himself commands ; that it leaves him a mere *pioneer* amid dangers and difficulties to which it may turn out that both he and his race are quite unequal, instead of a humble follower obeying the beckoning of one who holds both past and future in his hand.

And now as to my second point—that the very element which gives so beneficial a character to the belief that conscience is the inspiration of God—the very element which makes it a useful and practically stimulating belief, and not, as Prof. Clifford calls it, a mere source of "refined and elevated pleasure"—is also a note of its *truth.* I hold this to be so because the very experience which produces the trust is an experience of life, and of life morally higher than one's self. Surely, if we are competent, as we are, to say when our friends and our favourite books tempt us, and when they raise us above temptation, we are also competent to say when thoughts that strike with a living power upon the heart come from a higher and when they come from a lower source than that of our own habitual principles of action— when they come with promise and command, and when they come with discordant sneers, discouragement and enervation. When we grasp dimly at a great moral principle which is full, to use Prof. Tyndall's language, of "the promise and potency" of all forms of life—when the more we consider it, the less we see where it is leading us, and yet only feel the more confidence in it on that account—when we recognize a clue and a guide without recognizing where that clue and that guide are pointing to—when we know that it is our duty to defy the world in the name of a principle of which we cannot gauge the full meaning, or measure even the immediate effects (and this is as I maintain, the true phenomenon visible in all great moral, as in all great intellectual, origination)—then it does seem to me to be a sober and wholesome conviction that that which *we* do not know, there is one who puts the clue into our hands, who does know; that what we cannot foresee, there is one who does foresee; that we are grasping the hand of a Power which knows the way before as well as behind; that we are following the glimmer of a ray which will lead us on to the day-spring from which it descended. I cannot but believe that we have as secure a faculty to discriminate the superiority of the life in which a moral impression orginates as we have to discriminate its rightness itself—that it is one and the same act of discrimination which says, "This

is obligatory," and which says, "This is instinct with
divine life and promise." To suppose that a dead ances-
try are flashing though us these commands which at once
repudiate their principles and nerve us against the wrath
of their descendants, seems to me, I confess, a degrading
superstition. If " we boast to be better than our fathers."
It must be some one better than our fathers who is giving us our watchword. This is why I hold that to lose
the faith in God would be to lose a great inheritance of
moral order and moral progress, and also to lose at the
same moment a truth in comparison with which all other
truths are as dim and isolated sparks beside a pillar of
fire that can guide us though a wilderness that we have
never even explored.

SIR JAMES STEPHEN.

THE paper which began this discussion was entitled
" The Influence upon Morality of a Decline in Religious Belief." The Dean of St. Paul's remarks : "It seems to
me difficult to discuss this question till it is settled, at least
generally, what morality is influenced, and what religious
belief is declining." The Duke of Argyll observes that
these papers " deal with a question very abstract and
ill-defined." Dr. Ward says that " the wording of our
question is unfortunately ambiguous, and I think that
this fact has made the discussion in several respects less

pointed and less otherwise interesting than it might have been."

To these criticisms I reply that the title of my paper contains no question at all, and was not intended to do so. It is simply an indication, in the most general terms of the subject to which the paper of which it is the title relates. Any one who will take the trouble to read the paper will see that its principal object was to assert the proposition with which it concludes, which is in these words :

" This [i. e., the whole of the preceding argument] shows that the support which an existing creed gives to an existing system of morals is irrelevant to its truth, and that the question whether a given system of morals is good or bad cannot be fully determined until after the determination of the question whether the theology on which it rests is true or false. The morality is [I should have said " may be "] good if it is founded on a true estimate of the consequences of human actions. But if it is founded on a false theology it is founded on a false estimate of the consequences of human actions ; and, so far as that is the case, it cannot be good ; and the circumstance that it is supported by the theology to which it refers is an argument against, and not in favour of, that theology."

"The only "question" which my paper was intended to raise is the question whether that proposition is true or not ? I do not see how its truth can depend (as the Dean of St. Paul's suggests) upon further particulars as to "what morality is influenced," or "what theology is declining." I said nothing about the decline of any partciular theological belief, or its influence on any particular system of morals. My proposition would apply to all creeds and all forms of morality.

As to the Duke of Argyll's statement that "the question is very abstract and ill-defined," I should admit its justice if the title of the paper were taken as the statement of a question. But this is not the case. The proposition which I put forward, in the hope that it would be discussed, is no doubt general in its terms, but it seemed, and still seems to me, definite enough to be discussed. As to the "ambiguity" of which Dr. Ward complains, I cannot see how my proposition can have more meanings than one.

The papers which have been written subsequently to my paper raise a great variety of points which I feel much tempted to discuss, but I hardly feel at liberty to do so, as they do not in any way qualify anything said by me. Each paper, indeed, is an illustration of the truth of some part of my proposition or of the assertions by which it is introduced ; for each shows in various ways how very close is the connection in the writer's mind between the theological system which he believes to be true and the moral system which he considers to be good; and this, again, shows that the question of truth must precede the question of goodness, and cannot be determined by any answer which may be given to the latter question. I cannot help thinking that if this were understood generally it would affect very deeply the character of a great proionrpto of current theological speculation.

18